S0-FLR-286

The Butterfly Paperweight

by
Kayla Meyers

Publishing Room
1663 Liberty Drive, Suite 200
Bloomington, IN 47403
www.publishingroom.com
Phone: 1.877.655.1720

©2008. All rights reserved

No part of this book may be reproduced, stored in a retrieval system, or transmitted by any means without the written permission of the author.

ISBN: 978-0-9821-1311-0

First published by Publishing Room 8/15/08

Printed in the United States of America
Bloomington, Indiana

This book is printed on acid-free paper.

Faulty: Confessions of a Spina Bifida Patient

If anyone ever asks me what growing up was like for me I always tell them that I had the best and worst childhood imaginable. For the most part life at home was full of happiness, wonderment, fun and every day adventures. Looking back I cannot recall a single day when my mother, brothers and I weren't out somewhere having a fantastic time -- feeding geese and ducks on the small beach next to the Willamette River; riding the kiddie rides and wandering the grounds at the amusement park across the bridge in Portland; downtown Oregon City where she always let us go into the 99 cent store and pick out a toy (usually My Little Pony for me, while my brothers always got yo-yos or matchbox cars). Then we'd go up the Oregon City elevator and walk down the steps, circling around to the McLaughlin house where I would always request a penny to make a wish on and toss into the fountain. And if I wasn't out with my mom, then my twin brother and I were out with my grandmother. I was rarely home and even when I was I never stayed in the house for very long.

Our place was always full of kids because my mother ran a daycare from our house during the week. At one point she had thirteen kids plus her own three; I never ran out of friends to play with. The neighborhood was mostly boys at that time so I was constantly running after them, playing down in the creek in our backyard or playing with toy guns. I definitely fit in with the guys although I'm not entirely sure I'd fancy myself a real tomboy as I still loved all the little girly things. There were only two girls around my age that my mom looked after. We would sit in my room and play Barbies for hours. My room had two rather large closets that my mom and I shared. We'd empty her side and put on her clothes and prettify ourselves. I discovered the wonder of make-up then (which has since become a full-out addiction).

That portion of my life, at least, had absolutely nothing to do with the fact that I was sick. It's hard to explain because I was always very much *aware* of it, but when I was at home living my "normal" life it seemed to be a very minuscule, unimportant fact. A few rare times my illness would trickle over and interfere with my life; I've always had to catheterize myself and take antibiotics for the many infections I get. But they were more just little minor annoyances than anything big. What made a big difference in how I felt was that I was too young to understand that my life was somehow different from everybody else's. In my five-year-old brain I thought everyone visited the hospital frequently and had countless doctors.

From an outsider's perspective one may wonder how a little kid can cope with such an illness. But when you're on the other side of it there's nothing that feels really unique about being sick. It's just something in life that happens and you get used to it, simply deal with it and move on. No one in my family ever treated me like I was sick and none of my friends knew, so it was easy to push it aside even when I was dealing with it privately. It was like living a double-life, always treading softly the line between just trying to be a kid and being sick, desperately hoping they never intertwined. There was Plain Old Kayla and Kayla with Spina Bifida.

The other side of my childhood is a little more difficult while just as potent in my memory. For every summer day that I remember playing with my friends and discovering the world by my mother's side, I can just as easily describe to you innumerable hours spent in a doctor's office waiting to see yet another new specialist who supposedly had all the answers, or lying in a hospital with machines bleeping around me while people stood over me, poking and prodding and thumping. Doctors sat in front of me and discussed me as if I wasn't there, like I couldn't hear them marveling at how profoundly *abnormal* my body was, holding up charts and graphs that I couldn't read to help me understand. The sights, sounds, and smells of the medical world became very comfortable and familiar to me. The hospital was like a second home, and the people who cared for me during my visits became an extended family. Even today when I walk down the halls of Emanuel Hospital I am stopped by nurses, doctors, even the resident pastor as well as some janitors. (Seriously, janitors! My mom and I have a running joke that you know you've been in a hospital way too much when people who scrub the floor start to recognize you). Most of them have known me since I was just a toddler or younger, and I'm so grateful to have met so many wonderful people that are kind enough to remember me and be concerned. They remind me that goodness and genuine love do exist in this world. But even I have to admit, it was a lot for a little kid to process.

There was a great deal of fear, loneliness, and confusion in those first few years. Being in the hospital after surgery was tough, being away from my loved ones was difficult not to mention the slow and painful recuperation afterwards. Days in the hospital can be long and monotonous, even when you're family and friends come to visit. It all kind of blends into this blur of tests and updates and waiting. It was within the cold walls of those medical buildings as doctors came and dissected me like a frog in an eighth grade science class that I discovered something wasn't right about me.

It was in school, around first grade, that my illness became the most glaringly obvious. You know, kids like to ask lots of questions. Now I see that it wasn't cruelty but sheer curiosity that made them wonder how come I had to have my mother come to get me several times during the day for my periodic catheterizing regimen, or why I'd miss a half-day of school only to come back during lunch with cotton balls taped on my arms covering the marks from needles, or what happened to me when I'd leave for weeks and sometimes months at a stretch, then return sometimes in a cast or having bandages across my stomach with tubes still coming out of my side. They didn't get why I couldn't do everything they could, like some exercises in gym class, because my stamina and strength just wasn't up to par with theirs. It must have scared and confused them, I understand that now, but

I cannot even begin to express how uncomfortable and often downright humiliating it was for me at seven years old to have to explain the ins-and-outs of Spina Bifida to other little kids who just *didn't get it*. Up until then I'd lived in a world of doctors and hospitals and learned many things. I spoke the "doctor lingo" fluently and understood the various processes.

Discussing my health issues with my family was fine, but when I would talk with my friends, about the not-so-pleasant details they would scrunch up their nose in disgust. Finally I saw the separation between me and the other healthy kids, how our lives were just on totally opposite ends of the spectrum. For the first time I figured out that I *was* in fact different and, of course, no kid wants to be *different* from anyone else.

Adjusting to being around other, healthy kids was possibly one of the hardest times in my life, learning who I could trust and how much I could share, and what I should keep to myself. As cliché as this is going to sound, it was really a blessing in disguise because I discovered at a very young age how to spot a true friend and who really wasn't going to be there for me -- that doesn't mean it was easy or that it didn't break my heart a little when I lost someone who simply wasn't comfortable with being the friend of a girl who had medical problems, but I had to accept it anyway. It all taught me a lot about people as well as myself and ultimately shaped the person I've become. Back then I was horrified at the idea of somebody finding out I was sick, however today while I still don't go around broadcasting the fact that I was born with Spina Bifida if you're someone I know well enough to be sure I can trust you I'm a lot more open about the subject. After years of being ashamed of my "secret" life, it feels so great to be comfortable with it in the company of others and to know I don't have to hide who I am. Of everything I learned in school, that is the lesson I will remember the most. I think it has a lot to do with age and maturity-- kids are not going to be as open-minded as slightly older people will generally be, though I know plenty of people to whom that rule does not apply. Some people are eternally ten, but I digress.

As for the actual treatment of Spina Bifida, that's possibly the most complicated thing to explain. Spina Bifida is not a well-known, widely-understood birth defect, and it was even less so when I was growing up. The cause of it is still unknown (or merely not agreed upon, some doctors will tell you it has to do with how much folic acid the mother ingests while she is pregnant; others will tell you it's a random occurrence with no definitive warning-signs that a baby will or will not have it) and there is no cure. Besides that, it's very unpredictable because every case is different. There really is no one distinct course of action for treatment and much of what they do is experimental. Let me tell you, if I had a dollar for every time I've heard a doctor say, "Now there's no guarantee, but we just discovered this new pill/treatment/surgery and we're going to try it..." I'd be a millionaire. Also the effects of the illness are varied, from neurological to intestinal, and range in severity. Some children with Spina Bifida have more physical symptoms like being wheelchair bound or reliant on crutches, while others like me have no outward signs but all the internal damage. Because every case is entirely different from another and the symptoms are completely independent of the others you really have to treat each problem like its own individual thing.

Currently I have eight doctors; neurologists and neurosurgeons, gastroenterologist and urologists, orthopedists and specialists for the more specific problems that arise. Every one tells me something different, they all have their own approaches to dealing with it and opinions on what should be done. Often times they're wrong and I still run into problems that leave all of them absolutely, utterly stumped. To be perfectly honest, I learn something new about Spina Bifida with each new physician I saw. Of course you can imagine how frustrating it gets to never get a clearly distinct answer on what to do, you wish they'd all get together and have a big pow-wow and come to agreement on something but it doesn't happen. Sometimes they're spot-on, other times I wonder how I survive the crazy stuff they do to me. But ultimately, my best doctor is *me*; I've had this body for nearly 20 years and I know it better than anyone, so even when people are using me as a guinea pig and make uneducated guesses, I just have to listen to it and what it's telling me then let THEM know what they need to do. You'd be surprised how many times I've been right.

Growing up with Spina Bifida has been difficult and trying in many ways, but as I said it's such a large part of who I am today that I can't help but look at the overall picture in a positive light. I have always believed in the balance of life -- every positive has a negative, every negative a positive -- and while there have been some very hard things to deal with, I've also gained a lot of fantastic things from it. For a long time I struggled with the feeling that I was forced to grow up faster than

I should have, but now I'm glad that I learned so many valuable lessons at such a young age. I don't consider myself to be extraordinarily mature or wise, but I know I was better prepared to deal with other things that have come along and have a strength that I may have gained only much later in life, or not at all.

When people ask me what I think my life would be like if I wasn't born with Spina Bifida, and I physically shudder at the thought because I think without it I wouldn't even be *me*. That means that along with my illness I'd have to give up everything and everyone I hold dear in my life, and that's a trade I am not willing to make under any circumstances.

Private War

The most alone you could ever be,
Is being without yourself,
To stray so far outside of you,
There is no way to get back,
When you're lying alone in the dark,
And you feel so disconnected,
A blade pierces the flesh,
But you're already numbed with pain,
A friend says he'll be there for you,
Yet you're too frozen to reach out,
Even if you could explain,
There's nothing they could do,
No glue can paste together,
Pieces of a broken heart,
There is no needle or thread,
That can sew together shreds of the torn soul,
Human eyes are too blind to see,
Bruises beneath the skin,
Mortal ears are too deaf to hear,
Screams echoing from within,
Silent suffering is the worst kind of pain,
Because no one can help you through,
It's a private war you fight alone,
And most of the time you lose.

Chasing The Dragon

"Hey, do you mind?"
Zoning out had always been one of Gabriel's 'special talents'. From the time he was a kid, he had a knack for retreating inside himself and tuning everything out. Someone could be talking an inch from his face and he would just stare blankly right through him. He could hear nothing, see nothing, almost *feel* nothing. And it always seemed to happen at the most inopportune moments: during English class, during his grandmother's lectures, while a cop was reprimanding him for going on a joyride while intoxicated with his brothers. His mind was like a computer; after a while, he shut down and the screensaver popped up. A few years ago this ability to disconnect was aided by the great numbing elixir known as heroin. Back then, after he shot up a bomb could have been set off next to his head and he wouldn't have so much as twitched. But even now that he was sober – five years as of today, in fact – it was still just as easy for him to get lost inside the dark cave in his mind.

When her voice cut through his daze and entered his consciousness, he froze. Who could possibly be out here at this hour? No one should be awake this early in the morning besides except the birds and mice. His first instinct was to run. His eyes darted frantically left to right, anxiously searching for an escape route. The fence at the end of the alley stood roughly four feet high with forbidding, rusted barbed wire stretched across the top. Even if he could make it over without being caught, there was still the risk of getting his clothes snagged, or getting one nasty scrape. And a tetanus shot was not on his list of Things to Do Today. The other way was blocked by the dumpsters. He was trapped.

"Hey..." The voice said again. Besides the slight edge of irritation, the voice sounded completely non-threatening; it was soft, hesitant, and obviously female.

Slowly, he looked over.

The speaker was, indeed, a young girl. And even in this dim light, he could tell she was a very *beautiful* girl, at that. A petite little thing standing probably five-two at most and certainly not older than fifteen. She could definitely stand to gain five or even ten pounds; her green, low-cut t-shirt and long black skirt hung loosely on her thin body. No, *scrawny* was a better word for her, yet she had the beginnings of the curves of a woman. Her complexion was that of a porcelain China doll, not ashen and dull but creamy and flawless. The tiny freckles splayed across the bridge of her nose and cheeks were brought out by the slanted rays of sunlight dancing across her face. Her soft, full lips pouted naturally in a perfect bow, the color of brand new pink rosebuds in early spring. Long, bright, vibrant red hair hung over her shoulder in a twisted rope. As lovely as all her features were, most striking were her eyes; big, almond-shaped pools of emerald green with a ring of gold around the pupils. They studied him with innocent curiosity, yet something in them reflected a wisdom that far surpassed her childlike face and still developing body. Enchanting, captivating eyes…

"Do you mind?" She repeated.

He blinked, dumbfounded. "Huh?" Then he looked down and saw the pack of Marlboros he was still holding. "Oh, uh, yeah, sure…" he mumbled as he held the pack out to her.

"Thanks," she said, plucking a cigarette out of the pack.

He slipped the Marlboros back into his sweatshirt pocket and turned away from her again, taking nervously long drags on his own cigarette. When he looked back she was looking at him with one eyebrow cocked.

"What?" He asked, shifting uneasily on his feet.

She held up her unlit cigarette, raising her eyebrows even more. "Got a light?"

"Oh. Yeah," he replied stupidly. He reached back into his jacket and fished out his Zippo, surprised to find his hands shaking a little as he did so. He shielded the flame with a cupped hand as he held it out to her. Once the tip began to glow, he snapped the lighter closed and placed it back in his jacket.

He thought she would leave after that, but she didn't. He stood uncomfortably stiff, taking long drags and letting the burning nicotine fill his lungs, then releasing the smoke as slowly as possible. Maybe if he ignored her long enough and didn't make eye contact, she'd eventually lose interest. No such luck. Every time he looked back she was still standing there, staring at him with those mesmerizing, unnaturally green eyes.

He couldn't stand it anymore. He absolutely *hated* to be stared at, and he especially hated the way she was staring at him, as if she could see inside him. Ignoring her obviously wasn't working. Time for Plan B: Be as repulsive as possible.

"*What?*" He asked sharply, his irritation unmistakable. "Are you lost, little girl?"

She flinched at his tone, as if he'd physically struck her. "N-No, I was just... I'm Rhiannon," she told him quietly.

"That's nice," he said sarcastically.

She looked down for a moment, and then raised her head with determination. Well, she was persistent, he could give her that much.

"So... Where do you live? I don't think I've seen you before."

"Around," he replied shortly. By now he had smoked his cigarette down to the filter, and he cringed as it burned his fingers. He tossed it aside, stomped it out, and then immediately pulled out another.

"What's your name?" She tried again. She stood with her arms wrapped around her waist, but he figured it was due to being cold rather than modesty. Shy girls didn't wear plunging necklines in 17 degree weather. Moreover, shy girls didn't go bare *under* their plunging necklines.

"What are you, a decoy for the CIA?" He snapped, then sighed. "Look, maybe I don't have a name. Maybe mommy and daddy just didn't love me enough to name me, okay?" he told her, the sarcasm dripping from every word. "And speaking of mommy and daddy, yours are probably looking for you right now. You should run on home, kiddo."

"I'm not a child!" she said indignantly.

"Then, what are you? A hooker? Listen, sweetheart, you'll have to forgive me, because I'm not interested."

"I'm not a hooker, either! How *dare* you talk to me like that, you don't know *anything* about me!" she yelled. She threw her cigarette down, standing with her legs apart and balling her hands into fists so tightly that her knuckles turned white. To Gabriel she looked like a young, scrawny boxer who has just stepped into a ring with a seasoned fighter that clearly outweighed him by more than fifty pounds. It would have been funny, if she didn't have that killer's glare in her eyes.

He stared at her with his mouth open, shocked by her sudden outburst. Then he stepped forward, reaching out to touch her arm. "Whoa, sweetheart, calm down –"

"*Don't call me that!*" Rhiannon shouted, whirling around to face him.

Suddenly he found himself staring deep into those eyes, now alight with fiery anger. Her freckles stood out even more across her nose, hectic color flamed on the apples of her cheeks, her mouth pursed in a tight frown. Somehow, this way she was even more beautiful.

Gabriel stepped back, putting his hands up in a gesture of surrender. "Hey, okay. All right, just relax, sweet – I mean, it's Rhiannon, right? Rhiannon, I'm sorry."

She eyed him warily, still looking poised to attack.

"Gabriel," he admitted finally. "My name is Gabriel. Look, I really am sorry. I didn't mean to upset you." Well, yes, actually that's *exactly* what he meant to do. "You're right, I don't know you and I shouldn't have said those things."

The Butterfly Paperweight

She crossed her arms over her chest and stared at her feet.

"You, uh, dropped your cigarette. Want another?" He offered.

"No," she said quietly.

They stood in awkward silence until he thought of something to say.

"So, how old are you?" He cocked an inquisitive eyebrow at her. *Great, now you're trying to pick her up? Oh, you're a class act, Gabriel.*

"Nineteen," she told him with a little pride. "I'll be twenty in two weeks."

Nineteen? You've got to be kidding me. He thought about saying this aloud, then decided against it.

She seemed to read his mind and gave him a tiny smirk. "I know, I look a lot younger. But trust me, I'm older than you think." She added this last bit with a radiantly coy smile, winking at him.

He smiled back a little and started to speak when –

"*Rhiannon!*"

The gruff, unpleasant voice came from behind them, startling them both. Rhiannon stiffened, all of the color draining from her face.

"What's wrong?" Gabriel asked, frowning.

She motioned for him to be quiet then turned around, reluctantly walking out to the street.

"Rick?" She said timidly.

"*What are you doing?*" The angry voice came again. It sounded like grinding metal and make Gabriel cringe.

Suddenly, a man appeared near the opening of the alley where Rhiannon stood. He was tall and stocky with a shiny bald head. Rhiannon yelped as he seized her arms, roughly pulling her to him.

"*What* have I told you? Huh? You stupid girl," he growled lowly in her face. As he spoke he shook her furiously.

She whimpered in pain and cowered back, the image a far cry from the girl who looked ready to fight just moments before. "I-I'm sorry, I was just –"

He continued to shake her and berate her. His warm breath blowing billows of smoke in her face.

Gabriel straightened up and put his cigarette out, ready to go out and break them up. *It's none of your business. You know what happens when you butt in where you don't belong. Stay out of it,* a voice inside told him. Guiltily, he stood back and looked away.

At last she submitted and let him take her, leading her by the shoulders like a child. Before she disappeared she glanced in Gabriel's direction with a look of terror and desperation. He watched her go, shame churning in his stomach. And something else, another feeling he couldn't place. It came when she turned around for one last time, and he saw her frightened eyes. A feeling like déjàvu came over him.

After he finished his third cigarette, he walked out into the bright sunlight and headed back to his apartment. Subconsciously, he glanced back in the direction the man had dragged Rhiannon in.

World of Lies

The human eye is trained to see,
The image on the surface,
What people don't understand,
Is we have the ability to see deeper,
Our heart's eyes look through the lies,
Straight down to the bare truth,
Over time we just choose not to use our second sight,
Maybe because we're afraid to see what's really there,
Or maybe we just don't care to know,
But if we try we will come to another realm of understanding,
Where all our questions will be answered,
First though, we must look deep down into our own souls,
To find out whom we really are,
Because if we can't see our own truth,
How can we expect to see others?
It hurts us when people lie,
But all along we've been lying to ourselves,
We've chosen not to use our hearts,
To make our second set of eyes blind,
But they are still inside,
Waiting for the chance to reopen,
Next time you see someone smiling,
Take a second look,
If you do maybe then you'll see,
You're not the only one who's been hurting.

The Broken Ones

The next morning her thoughts and feelings had returned completely. Before she opened her eyes she was aware of a deep, burning pain in her lower arms. White bandages coiled around her arms from wrist to elbow. White, everything here was blindingly white: the bare, uncongenial walls, the neatly pressed sheets that had the faint smell of ammonia, the curtains that framed the small window to her left. There was only a single item that was colored was a faux-leather chair next to her bed. It was dark, crimson red.

Her fingers skimmed over the raised bars that encased her on both sides. She was tied down by leather traps that were hooked with metal buckles around the bar handles.

"Just a precaution," a sweet, quiet voice told her.

Startled, Cleo whirled around toward the doorway. A young, pretty woman in sea-foam green scrubs was positioned half in the room and half in the hall.

"To make sure you can't hurt yourself again."

"Who are you?" Cleo asked. There was nothing threatening about the woman, but Cleo was afraid of her anyways.

"I'm Leanne, a nurse on the West Psychiatric Ward."

Psychiatric ward? Cleo thought. Then she saw the suitcases sitting by the chair. "I have to stay here?"

"Your parents and the doctors have decided that it's in your best interest for us to keep you here until we can evaluate you and decide how we can help you," Leanne explained as she walked over and unbuckled the straps. After Cleo was partially free, Leanne began unplugging all the machines she'd been hooked up to.

Evaluate *me? Like I'm some kind of newfound species of reptile they've captured, and now they're bringing in experts to poke and prod at me from behind glass and document their findings?* Call it foolish pride, but more than anything she was insulted by the idea. She wasn't about to be made into a chapter in a mass-produced textbook to be studied in college psychology classes. "Don't I have a say in anything?" Cleo asked.

Leanne gave her a sympathetic little smile that Cleo didn't like. "I'm sorry, but no. You're a minor and your parents have the authority to decide whether or not you should be hospitalized."

There it was, that word: *hospitalized*. It made her shiver the way it was so casually said, how carelessly it was thrown into her face. Yet, hearing it so plainly stated was strangely liberating as well. Deep inside she felt an odd sort of relief that it was finally put on the table. She was being *hospitalized*.

"How long?" Cleo asked while slowly pushing herself upright. Her muscles felt weak, like it was the first time she'd used them in months.

"Initially, thirty days," Leanne replied matter-a-factly, as she clamped off the IV in Cleo's hand. "Then, we'll re-evaluate your case and decide whether or not you can be released."

A month- the perfect amount of time for all her friends to figure out what really happened to poor, little Cleo. Just long enough for word to spread that she had gone insane and been thrown into a padded cell somewhere upstate. Enough time for her entire world to fall apart.

"As you can see, your parents came by this morning while you were still asleep to drop off some things for you," Leanne continued. "I'll show you the bathroom so you can take a shower, if you want. Then I'll take you to your new room."

A shower sounded great to Cleo. She found a change of clothes and then followed Leanne down the hall to the shower. She kept her eyes to the floor as they walked down the long, bright hallway, avoiding the curious glances of the other patients and nurses. She could imagine what they must be thinking: *Look at this, guys, we got another one... Another spoiled, attention-starved little girl who just couldn't bear her perfect world of designer clothes and fancy cars. So one night she decides to play with daddy's razor to end her suffering. So instead of finding sweet nirvana— she ends up in here with us. Well, sweetheart, what do you think? Is it everything you wanted? Better get used to it, you're going to be here for a long, long time...* She hurried to catch up with Leanne, suddenly feeling like the walls were shrinking in around her. And those voices, the laughter she couldn't hear but she could *feel*. She felt sick.

Leanne must have sensed her distress, because she turned abruptly and put her arms out as if to catch her. "Are you all right? Do you feel dizzy? If you don't feel well, I can take you back to your room and you can shower later. You lost a lot of blood, and –"

"I'm fine," Cleo interrupted, weakly. Grayness threatened to steal her sight. She gripped the railing on the wall and pushed it away.

Leanne giving her an uneasy look, nodded and unlocked the bathroom by punching in a code on a keypad next to the door. The room was like a cylinder-block closet with a toilet, sink, and shower stall that reminded Cleo of the girls' locker room at school. The hospital also took the 'precaution' of having someone watch you while you showered. It was humiliating to have someone there with only a sheer curtain to keep her from being totally exposed. Shutting her eyes tightly, she tried to imagine being at home in that bathroom of hideous blue-and-white, the wooden Dorothy wall ornament smiling down at her from her place on the wall. She could almost smell her lavender shampoo, and the jasmine candle that was always burning. For once, the thought of home actually comforted her.

"Are you almost finished?" Leanne's voice cut through Cleo's thoughts.

Cleo opened her eyes, and once again was back in the coldness of the small hospital bathroom. Taking as much time as possible, she dried off, dressed and followed Leanne back to her room.

"Can I help you with something?" the nurse asked while Cleo got her things.

"No," Cleo said quickly, hugging the bags closer to her body.

Leanne nodded understandingly, giving her that same pitying smile. Cleo shifted her eyes downward and stared at the floor. The nurse motioned for her to follow and they began making their way to Cleo's new room. Her new room *on the psyche ward.*

This can't be happening, her mind insisted as she trailed after Leanne. *This **cannot** be happening…*

Walking into the main building beyond the doors marked 'Critical Care' was like stepping into an entirely different world. It was much brighter and surprisingly colorful. The walls were a dusty rose pink with a flowered border at the top, the floors toffee-colored marble tiles. Warm sunlight poured through the large windows on either side of her. Outside she could see the autumn-colored leaves trembling and swaying gently and thought of how wonderful the soft breeze would feel on her skin. A gentle rain had begun, pattering against the windows temptingly. Below she could see people on the sidewalks with umbrellas and newspapers over their heads, rushing to get inside. City traffic was sluggish as usual, cars pulling out of the hospital parking lot and disappearing off into the horizon. Silently, Cleo felt a dismal sort of envy and contempt for them all – they carelessly took for granted their freedom, showing no empathy or concern for the ones who couldn't leave. But, hadn't she done the same thing? Isn't that why she was here in the first place? Really, she was just like them, a realization which only served to dishearten her even more.

The hallways twisted and turned in a confused pattern, all seeming to lead everywhere and nowhere in particular. As they walked endlessly from one corridor to another, Cleo began to feel like a lab rat in a 3-D maze seeking its cheese.

Marked signs with painted arrows were the only indication of where she was going: Up led to Day Surgery, Left was Pediatrics, Right to Diagnostics. There were doors on both sides of her, some offices with doctors' names on them, others waiting rooms where families huddled together on the uncomfortable-looking chairs. Eventually they came to a second ward like the one she was in, and even before they walked inside she knew where they were. The sign above the door said Pediatric Oncology. As she stepped through the door, she was immediately struck by a wretched smell that washed over her like a tidal wave. She recognized it from the nursing home that her grandmother had been in when she was a little girl – it was the musty, stale odor of a place where people were dying. But the ones dying here were not eighty-or-ninety year olds with graying hair. These were young kids, some looking all of a day past five, in wheelchairs or pushing IV poles alongside them. Most of them had no hair. They stared at her as they walked by, and she knew she would see their sunken, hollow eyes in her dreams for the rest of her life.

Inside the last room in the hall Cleo saw a little girl lying in the bed with machines around her. Her light brown hair wasn't completely gone, but it was thin and patchy. In her arms she held a brown and black teddy bear that was holding a red heart. As they walked by the little girl's dim, tired hazel eyes opened and shifted toward Cleo. Her eyes were angry. *Do you see?* Her bitter expression asked. *You're here because you **chose** it, and why? Because it wasn't **enough** for you, because you wanted something more. You'll never have any idea what it's like to* *be me. You made your choice, and I sure hope it was worth it. Look at me, what choice do **I** have?*

Cleo looked away in shame, tears burning her eyes. She had to get away from the knowing eyes. Everything was closing in around her, she wanted to scream. She walked closer to Leanne, almost running now.

"It's hard, isn't it?" Leanne said as she unlocked the door at the end of the corridor.

Cleo looked up, surprised. "What?"

"Being here," Leanne said, waving her hand around. "Seeing the kids sick like this. It makes you think about things differently."

After more twists and turns, Leanne led her to a room done in soft pastel yellow. The beds did not have bars or shackles on them, but instead had brightly colored sheets . The bed next to hers was made up in vibrant pink. The little desk next to it was covered in knick-knacks.

"As you can see, you have a roommate. Don't worry, you'll love her," Leanne told her as they walked in.

Don't count on it, Cleo thought to herself. She almost said it out loud, but bit her tongue. She just wanted to be alone right now, so whatever she could say to get Leanne out was fine by her. "Okay."

"You can settle in tonight. Tomorrow you're going to have some visitors, staff mostly," Leanne explained as she took Cleo's bags from her and set them on the bed.

"Visitors?"

"Staff, mostly, just –"

"Standard procedure," Cleo finished for her.

Leanne smiled. "Dinner is in a little while if you're hungry, and I'll be down the hall so you can buzz me if you need anything, okay?"

"Thanks," Cleo said softly.

As Leanne turned to leave, she looked back at Cleo and smiled "Cleo...It *will* be okay. I know it seem like it right now, but it will be soon," Leanne promised her.

Cleo didn't believe Leanne, but she was grateful to her for trying. In spite of herself, she was starting to like Leanne. She nodded and gave the nurse her best smile.

After Leanne was gone, Cleo sat on the bed with her back pressed against the wall, her knees pulled up to her chest and resting her head on them. In the silence, reality came crashing down on her. This *was* really happening. She was really here in this place surrounded by all these people who didn't know her, and didn't care. With her family and friends miles away, she realized how more than anything else, she felt alone. She was so lost in her thoughts that she didn't even hear the door open again.

"Hi!" A voice chirped.

Cleo groaned inwardly, *Oh, God, what now?* Couldn't everyone just go away and let her feel sorry for herself? She finally looked up reluctantly, her vision blurred with tears.

Sitting on her bed uncomfortably close to her was a girl who Cleo guessed was about her age, with bright blue eyes and bouncing light blonde curls. She didn't seem to notice that Cleo was crying, but just simply grinned even wider at Cleo's acknowledgement. Her teeth were pearly white and perfectly rounded, giving her the impish look of a sprightly young child.

"They refer to me as the manic-depressed girl, but my name is Arianna – *Ah-ri*, not *Airy*," she told Cleo, and giggled. Cleo had a feeling she'd made this introduction several times before.

"Hi," Cleo said flatly, wiping at her eyes.

"What's your name?" Arianna asked, sitting cross-legged next to Cleo like best friends sharing a secret.

"Cleo."

"Like Cleopatra?" Arianna said excitedly.

Like she hadn't heard *that* a millions times in her life. She had to resist the urge to roll her eyes, reminding herself that Ari didn't know it was one of her biggest pet-peeves. "No, not like Cleopatra. I was named after the ."

Arianna wrinkled her nose, as if she didn't understand or wasn't satisfied by this. "Oh, I like Cleopatra better. So, anyway, what did you do to get yourself in here, Cleo?"

Cleo lifted up her sleeve to let Arianna see the bandages.

"Ah, yeah, I did that once, too," she said, and showed Cleo the horizontal scars on her wrists. "I think that was my... Let's see, once when I was thirteen, once when I was fifteen... I guess about my fourth try, almost one year ago now."

Cleo gaped at her, horrified. "You've been here a *year?*"

"Next month, officially. My parents kicked me out, and I'm too old to go into foster care, so I really don't have anywhere else to go. Kind of sucks, but it could be worse, I guess," she sighed and leaned back on her elbows. She narrowed her eyes at Cleo thoughtfully. "Why did you do it?"

Cleo shifted uncomfortably. All morning she'd been asking herself the same question, and she hadn't been able to come up with a good answer yet. "I...I don't know," she replied shyly, and felt herself welling up again.

"Well, don't worry, I'm sure one of the geniuses in here can tell you," Ari told her with a roll of her eyes. Then she tapped Cleo on the knee. "Hey, come on, it's dinnertime. I'll introduce you to everybody."

Meeting *everybody* didn't sound very appealing to Cleo. "I'm not hungry," she said, which was only partially true. It occurred to her that she hadn't eaten for the past two days, and while the idea of food wasn't appealing, she *was* hungry.

"Aw, come on, you can't just sit around here all day, you'll go crazy...Well, you know, I mean you'll go *crazier*," Ari corrected herself and laughed again.

Cleo didn't return the laugh, but Ari wasn't bothered. "Let's go," she pulled Cleo up and started leading her toward the door. "They're going to start thinking we actually *did* kill ourselves..."

Cleo sighed deeply and followed after her. She had a feeling it was going to be a long month.

Masquerade

Played my part again in the masquerade
Filled in the cracks, painted a smile on my face
I danced again the deceitful waltz, hid my soul in disgrace
All around me I see the masks of Cheshire grins and lying eyes
And I know they can see I don't belong in this world
Of perfection and empty fantasies

What can I do and what can I say
To fool my heart again today?
If I repeat the words, if I just pretend
Will you believe that I'm okay?
The mask is chipped, falling from my face
But if I smile, bid the pain away
Maybe I'll fool myself someday

Painted illusions and pretty words
Chase me in my sleep, as the phantoms scream inside my dreams
The lie is melting, colors drip down the walls
And without the veneer, where can we hide?
Stain glass windows break, scattering on the floor
And there's nowhere left to go, 'cause we can't tell what's real anymore

Well I don't care if it's destroyed, this place of unreality
Ashes to ashes, dust to dust
It all comes to an end anyway
All I want is all that's real
The flaws and tatters in my soul
Don't care if I'm right, if it's illogical
All I want is something real

Goodbye, September

His bags were packed and sitting in a jumbled heap by the front door. The sky outside was growing increasingly dark from the storm clouds that were drifting in from the south. Elongated shadows sprawled throughout the eerily quiet house, leaving the home with a cold bleakness. The air was unnervingly still and thick. Everything was silent except the sound of soft, rhythmic drumming of raindrops on the rooftops and pattering against the windowpanes like idle hands on a tabletop. It was as if the world was holding its breath as it waited for inevitable disaster to strike.

He and his wife were upstairs in their bedroom, neither of them speaking. He was standing in front of the dresser mirror, fastening the buttons on his green army shirt. Seeing his impassive, composed face made her feel like crying all over again. She forced herself to look away. She turned her attention towards the yellow and white comforter. Her fingers traced over the raised stitches that created a pattern of roses and baby breath. His mother gave it to them as a wedding present five years ago. It seemed the most integral events in their married life had occurred around, on top, or beneath the soft plush fabric. They spent their first night as husband and wife was spent on this bed, under this comforter. Their first marital squabble had taken place in the bedroom; which was later resolved beneath this blanket. He'd sat next to her on this bed when she'd received word that she was getting promoted at work, and spent the night covering her in kisses. And finally, just last week, he came home to find her sitting on the bed crying as she clutched a piece of crumpled paper to her chest. The piece of paper was to inform them that he was being deployed to Iraq for the next year.

He turned toward her. Her eyes were fixed on the place where he'd slept next to her every night for the last five years. He watched her restless fingers move across the embroidered flowers, her nail snagging a few stitches here and there, causing them to begin to fray. Looking at her made his chest tighten; he fought against the strong current of emotion, struggling to keep a hold of his composure. She hadn't been eating or sleeping. Her face was pale and deep purple circles had formed under her eyes. It was a habit she'd developed to cope with stress. In the past five years, her anxiety had seemed to subside and she hadn't needed to resort back to it as means to calm her nerves. Until now. He knew he was the cause of it and it broke his heart.

He walked towards her. She remained motionless at first, and then slowly, she sat up. For the first time that day, their eyes met. He leaned down to pull her near but she resisted, pulling back. Her eyes roamed over him, taking in every curve and bend and freckle. Eventually her eyes settled back on his. They gazed wordlessly. He tried again to draw her close, and this time she allowed him. A thousand kisses had been shared between them; passionate, tender, sweet, but none like this one. Even in their embrace, with their lips planted firmly together, they could both feel the separation happening between them. Her lips were not loving or affectionate but only desperate. His fingers were the same, grasping her not in desire but in the frantic, hopeless way a man at the edge of a cliff clings to a slippery rope. It was the only thing left for them to do; a final kiss: a good-bye kiss.

When they released their embrace, they stared deep into each others eyes. She studied the flecks of color in his eyes. She ripped her eyes from his. She looked down. "Your boots are going to ruin the carpet," she told him indifferently. "We spent a lot of money on this carpet."

"I know," he said as he dug his heels deeply into the floor. The black marks he left would never come out. *Good,* he thought. *Let it go to hell. Who cares, anyway?*

She wiped away her tears. "It's raining; don't forget to put on your jacket before you leave. It will probably be cold on the plane."

"I will," he said.

"Did you call your mother?" she asked.

He pressed his lips to hers, cutting her off. She squeezed him tightly as she buried her face in his neck. He held her one last time beneath the comforter, and when it was over they laid next to each other without touching. He slowly turned and raised his head, looking at the digital alarm clock on the nightstand. He nudged her, she knew it was time. They got up, got dressed and made their way downstairs. They walked out into the dreary afternoon. He put his things in trunk of the car before climbing into the drivers seat. The rain continued as they drove, and by the time they reached the airport, it had turned into a torrential down-pour. Angry gusts of wind pushed the tiny pebbles of hail in a downward slant, the bits of ice hammering on the hood.

"I'll call whenever I can," he said, his voice barely audible above the pounding of the rain on the car. "Do you have the address to write to me?"

"Yes," she said flatly. She refused to meet his eyes, instead looking straight ahead into the stormy afternoon. "You're going to miss your flight."

He exhaled deeply and reached over, lightly squeezing her arm. She didn't move. Neither of them said 'I love you'. He got out and gathered his things from the trunk, and made his way toward the building. She watched as he disappeared into the crowd. Outside, the sleet pounded harder on the roof of the car, echoing hollowly in her ears. Suddenly, she realized he'd left his black hooded jacket on the seat beside her. She grabbed it and started to run after him. But he was already gone. She stood there with his jacket in her hands. She ran her fingers over the soft material, bringing it up to her nose, she inhaled long and deep, taking in the faint smell of his cologne. Slowly, she pulled it over her head and began her long journey home, alone.

Before You
By: Joshua Rheaume and Kayla Meyers

Every day in this cold and gray, lonely world
The colors blend and time collides.
Don't know how or why or when
My soul is bare, I'm dead inside.
Nothing anymore to make me feel alive.

Before you, before I saw your face
And the light of your smile, like the warmth of a thousand
Burning suns, electricity radiating through my soul
And I realize there was never any life.
I was never quite alive, before you
Before you.

I never saw a sunset before, the depth of the night
The rose never bloomed, all the stars did not shine for me.
Now the world breathes again, and time has stopped.
Oh, I can't explain how everything changed, since I heard
your voice.

Before you, before I saw your face
And the light of your smile, like the warmth of a thousand
Burning suns, electricity radiating through my soul.
And I realize there was never any life.
I was never quite alive, before you-
Before you.

This was written at the request of my very close friend, Joshua Rheaume. He then took my words and recorded them as a song which he later put on his website. It turned out wonderfully and will soon be digitally released under TzR Records. I am very happy and proud to have collaborated with him on it. This piece is dedicated to him.

Introduction –
The Kate and Stephen Series

The following stories, *Time Wasted* and *Craving*, are part of a series that chronicles the relationship of Stephen Braithwaite and Katelyn Ackerly. This is the journey of two people through love, addiction, and the choices they make when faced with the reality of both.

Time Wasted

When Kate Ackerley met Stephen Braithwaite, they were both into the college party scene. Just past twenty-one, they were living on their own for the first time. With no responsibilities, they were eager to experience this foreign idea of freedom. Days were spent in lecture halls listening to professors drone on about things they didn't particularly care about. They lived for the nights, the bars and the scene. Their freshly laminated IDs got their fair share of usage as they sampled everything from cheap beer to the expensive wines. It was a rite of passage, and with no one around to stop them, they were free to run as wild as they wanted without consequence. And they took full advantage of it.

It was because of alcohol that Kate and Stephen met. If on that fateful Saturday night she'd decided to stay back at the dorm to study instead of giving into her friends' prodding, and if he'd gone home instead of making just one more stop, they would never have seen each other. But, as it happened, they did end up in the same club, and just as Kate decided it was time for her to leave, Stephen was on his way to the bar to order another drink.

The result of their collision was a ruined satin dress and shattered glass.

"I-I'm sorry..." He stammered as he bent down to pick up the broken remains of the glasses he was carrying. He saw the dark stain trickling down the front of her dress, seeping into the fabric. "Oh, God... I'm so sorry... Here..." He quickly grabbed a few napkins from the table beside them, beginning to blot her skirt.

She grunted, a mix of revulsion and humor. "It's all right. I never liked this dress anyway, my mother sent it to me," she told him while stooping down to help him clean up the mess. "Are *you* all right? Did you cut yourself on the glass?"

He smiled a little as he watched her, admiring the way her light brown hair cascaded down over her shoulder. "No, I'm okay."

After picking up everything she could find, Kate straightened up to find Stephen checking her out. She gave him a smile, blushing furiously. "Hi. I'm Kate, but pretty much everyone calls me Katie even though I despise it – it makes me feel like a little gap-toothed seven year old in a flowered dress and pigtails. Kate is fine."

He laughed. "It's nice to meet you Kate. I'm Stephen."

She smiled. The skin around her eyes crinkled at the corners, evidence of the all-night study sessions on the eve of an exam or writing thesis papers. She had all the usual symptoms of an overworked, exhausted college student, but her slightly disheveled appearance somehow made her even prettier.

"Stephen," she repeated. "Nice to meet you."

"Are you in a rush to leave, or will you let me make this little accident up to you and buy you another drink?" He asked

Kate chewed her lip thoughtfully, glancing over his shoulder at the door. Typically she wasn't the kind of girl to follow after someone who she'd just met, but she didn't like the idea of going home by herself either. He seemed nice enough, and he was the only person to speak to her all night since her friends abandoned her in favor of a group of fraternity boys.

*And, come on, just **look** at him. You'd be a damn fool to pass this up*, the youthful indiscretion in her mind argued. She looked back at him and nodded. "No rush, a drink sounds great."

He grinned and took her arm in his, leading her to a booth in the back. They drank while they chatted in the easy manner of long-time friends. By the end of the night, Kate found herself climbing into the front seat of his Mazda, allowing him to bring her back to his place. She awoke the next morning at his side. They opted to skip classes that day, and soon Kate realized that she was beginning to fall for Stephen.

In those first weeks of being together, they were like any young love-stricken couple: Kate spent more and more time at his place during the week. She was glad that she finally had someone to go out with instead of always playing tag-along with her unreliable girlfriends. They were free to go and do as they please. He made her laugh, and there was something about him that made her feel at home. She felt comfortable and secure around him. It didn't matter where they were or what they were doing, if he was there with her she was more than content – he'd fast become the best friend she'd had since moving here.

It took over a month for Kate to notice something that there was something not quite right with Stephen. She began to understand that whenever they went out, he wasn't there simply to have a good time, but rather on a mission to leave completely drunk. She and her friends were known to let loose, but they generally knew their limit and stopped just short of going too far. But Stephen didn't appear to *have* a limit. Long after the others had cut themselves off he would stay at the bar, practically drinking the place dry. Kate would attempt to pull him away, but his already stubborn nature was only magnified by intoxication and it always ended in an argument.

Eventually he would become too drunk to fight which allowed Kate to get him home, clean him up and put him to bed. It bothered her, but she never voiced any of her concerns to him. Whenever she felt on the edge of her breaking point, she rationalized with herself: she drank too, so did all of their friends. She was his girlfriend, not his mother – it was her responsibility to love him and be there when he needed her, not judge him or scold him.

He would eventually reach a point where he'd decide he needed to settle down, and things would be fine. It would happen soon enough, all she had to do was ride it out until then.

Things only worsened as time went on. Soon Stephen's drinking was more than just weekend fun. Kate began to find bottles of hard liquor and wine hidden in various places around the house; he was drunk more often than he was sober. Kate tried talking with him, but he

The Butterfly Paperweight

completely denied that he had a problem, telling her she was overreacting. His behavior became more erratic and worrisome over time, until Kate began to hate going out with him. Sober, he was kind and gentle, never raising his voice or losing his temper, but under the influence his quiet self-assurance turned into complete arrogance. He became unhinged. Many evenings resulted in full-on brawls with Stephen at the center of it. Kate was becoming increasingly embarrassed and hurt by his actions. Each night ended with her face buried in her hands, tears of humiliation streaming down her cheeks.

One night after Kate and her best friend helped a belligerent Stephan to bed, Jess had taken all she could swallow.

"Kate, this has to stop," Jess told her gently. "He can't keep doing this to us, and especially to you. What happens if one time he ends up hurting *you*? He's not the same when he drinks, you can't trust him."

Angry, Kate quickly stepped back, glaring at her friend. "Stephen would never hurt me. Ever. He may get a little out of control sometimes, but he loves me, and he wouldn't lay a finger on me. He just wouldn't, Jess."

Kate ran into the house. She made it to the bottom of the steps before her knees gave out and she sank to the ground. The tears streamed from her tired eyes. With all her heart she wanted to believe what she'd told Jess, but something inside told her she was wrong.

It wasn't until a few months later that Stephen did hurt Kate. It was the second to last week of December. They'd been invited to a Christmas party; as Kate finished the final touches of makeup Stephan did a couple of shots. . As always, Kate was concerned about getting in a car with him, especially when there was a fresh coating of snow covering the ground, but he was impossible to reason with. They had made it there all in one piece, but an argument had brewed in the car ride over. Kate had wanted to go home to spend Christmas with her family, and it was a source of contention prior to the car ride. The argument carried over into the party. How she wished she wouldn't have said anything. Stephan headed toward the bar to calm his nerves as soon as they arrived. But the alcohol only mad it worse. His anger boiled over and he began to yell at her. The commotion was enough to make everyone in the room stop and watch them.

"Will you keep your voice down?" Kate whispered harshly, her face flushed.

With those words, Stephen's patience broke; before she had a chance to move his hand was landing on her face with a loud smack. A stir of horrified gasps echoed throughout the room. The force of the wallop sent Kate backwards as her hand grasped her throbbing face. More than anything, what frightened her was the absolute blackness in his eyes – there was no apology, no remorse whatsoever, only pure contempt and rage.

She could feel everyone's eyes on her, pitying her, judging her and thinking how incredibly stupid she must be for allowing this to happen. Quickly she bolted from the room, darting into the bathroom. She hunched over the sink and cried, she cried until her stomach churned and she threw up. An hour later when she finally emerged, pale with mascara running down her face and the bruise on her cheek deepening to dark purplish-blue, she saw Jess standing there waiting for her.

"Jess," she sobbed, fighting to gain composure. "*Please* just… Don't say 'I told you so', okay?"

Jess hugged Kate tightly and wiped the black streaks off her face. Jess looped her arm around Kate's waist and took her out to the car, and drove her home. When they got back to the house that Kate and Stephen shared, Jess took Kate inside and led her up to the bedroom. The girls sat together on the bed while Jess held an ice pack to Kate's cheek.

Kate's began to subside a while later, tapering off into small whimpers. "I'm sorry, Jess…" She whispered. "I'm sorry I didn't listen to you…"

"Look at me, Kate," Jess said as she raised Kate's chin so she could look in her eyes. "You don't have to be sorry for *anything*, okay? This was not your fault, so don't you dare apologize for something *he* did. This was on Stephen, not you. Understand?"

Kate nodded slowly, breaking down again. She buried her face in Jess' shoulder and cried herself to sleep. Jess stayed with her for a while, then put Kate in bed and left. As she was leaving, Stephen pulled in and came walking up the driveway. He could barely stand up let alone walk straight. Jess stopped him.

"Get out of here, Stephen," she told him firmly. "Kate doesn't have anything to say to you, and neither do I for that matter."

"Look, Jess," he slurred, faltering a bit and catching himself on the hood of his car. "I know I made a mistake–"

"Damn right, you did," she retorted angrily. "Who the hell do you think you are? What gives you the right to blacken my friend's eye, and then come back here?"

Stephen gritted his teeth. "Get out of my way, Jess. I just need to talk to her."

"Oh, that's it, huh? That's how you're going to fix this, by talking to her? Tell her that you're so *sorry*, then maybe you can go out and buy her some make-up to cover the bruise she's going to have to walk around with for the next three weeks, if it ever fully heals." Then she caught sight of the way he was clenching his fists at his side. "What are you going to do now, hit me?"

He acted like he would lash out and strike her, but then his expression slowly changed and he let his arms go lax. Jess never moved, she continued to look at him steadily. A second before he turned away, she almost thought she could see tears in his eyes.

"I don't know what I'm doing half the time anymore, Jess," he confessed. "Suddenly, I feel like everything is slipping through my fingers but I can't stop it from happening. Kate is the best thing in my life, the only good thing I've had in a long time. How could I let things go so far that I put our relationship in jeopardy?"

Jess let her breath out slowly, relaxing a little. "Just leave her alone for tonight, okay? Go somewhere and sober up, then come back and talk it over with her. She needs time right now, and I think you do, too. You both need to figure out how you're going to handle this. You know how Kate is – I'm sure in a little while she'll be willing to listen and forgive you."

"But you don't think she should, do you?" He asked.

"No," she answered bluntly. "But this is Kate's decision, not mine."

"Can I stay here for tonight?" He asked, looking up at her with a little smile.

She laughed. "I don't think so. But, I'll drive you to a motel."

"Thanks, Jess."

"You're welcome," she started to walk to her car, but then stopped to look back at him. "But if you ever touch her again, I'll kill you. Got it?"

"I promise. Never again."

'Never again' was approximately three months later. Stephen fell deeper and deeper into the abyss of his addiction until soon it consumed his entire life; when he woke up, he drank. Before he left for school he drank, when he got home he drank. Kate would beg him to stop, even threaten to leave if he didn't. The routine was always the same, Stephen would break down, apologize and swear he would change.

He'd make an effort to change, but it never lasted long. Even when he went back to his normal routine she would stay. Not because of denial or stupidity but because she had faith in Stephen, a faith so deep and strong that even if she wanted to wouldn't allow her to walk away. Most of all, she couldn't let go of the hope that, if no one else could, she would be the one to save him.

Things continuously got worse. It was a Tuesday when Kate finally realized how bad things really were. She went to her morning classes, like normal and then came home on her lunch break to run some errands. An envelope from her mother was lying on the counter. It was opened. The letter read "I know money is tight, I hope this helps" But there was no money in the envelope. Kate's heart began to pound. How could he?

Without hesitating she grabbed her jacket and ran back to her car, driving to the bar on the corner of the street. When she walked in she saw Stephen. A guy had pinned him against the wall, and from the doorway she could see that Stephen's nose was bleeding heavily.

"Dear God..." She moaned under her breath, her eyes filling with tears.

She ran over, pushing her way through the crowd that was surrounding the men, finally reaching Stephen who had managed to wriggle free and was now dominating the fight. "Steve, no! Come on, babe, stop–"

An incoherent, angry Stephen whipped around suddenly, knocking Kate back with his elbow. Kate staggered backward, tripping on the feet of the spectators and fell into the bar, smacking the back of her head into the corner. The last thing she heard was a commotion of voices and running footsteps, and in the distance the sound of police sirens.

When Kate awoke she was lying in a hospital bed with Jess by her side. She squinted her eyes against the brightness of the lights and touched her forehead. Pain shot through her eyes, she yanked her fingers away quickly, groaning.

Jess's arms were crossed and she was shaking her head. Jess just sat there silently. "Jess, this was –"

"Save it, Katie, I've heard it; it was a mistake, right? Just a little accident?"

Kate sighed. "You just don't—"

"Understand?" Jess interrupted coldly. "Oh, you're right, I don't. I don't understand how my best friend who I've seen as one of the most intelligent, level-headed women I know, could stay with a man who shoves her around."

The Butterfly Paperweight

Kate didn't answer. She pulled her legs up and buried her face, her shoulders trembling. "I'm sorry…" she cried, her voice muffled.

Jess sat forward and raised Kate's chin. "You don't have to be sorry, because you didn't do anything wrong. This is his battle, and you shouldn't have to fight it for him. It's his choice, not yours – You can't save him, not by yourself. He needs help now that you can't give him."

Kate pulled back, turning away. "I need to be by myself for a little bit."

Jess stood up without another word and walked to the door. Before she left, she turned back to Kate one last time. "There's room for you at my place whenever you need somewhere to stay."

Kate watched her go without saying anything, then curled up on her side and cried herself to sleep.

She was released two days later. She didn't call Stephen to say when she was coming home although he'd left her about twenty messages, begging for her forgiveness. Instead she took a bus home and found the house empty, which she was glad for.

Kate went upstairs, found her suitcases in the closet and began folding up her clothes. After everything she could fit in her bags was packed away, she called Jess and left a message to say that she would accept the room if it was still open. Looking up at the clock, she calculated that Stephen would be off work in a little over an hour. Just long enough for her to do what she had to.

Putting her bags down by the door, she went into the kitchen and found a pen with a few pieces of paper, then sat down in the living room. It was more difficult than she thought, and she erased and scratched out things as she went along, having to stop a few times for another piece of paper because the other had been stained by tears. Finally she finished and tacked it up on the wall by the front door where she knew it would be seen.

Doubling-checking to make sure not to forget anything, she gathered her things in her arms, reaching for the doorknob. Before she did she turned once more, looking around the empty apartment. The quiet flushing of the central air was all she could hear. She took in the sight of everything slowly, the bits and pieces of the life she was leaving behind; the brand new furniture they'd gone out looking for together, art pieces they'd bought from neighboring towns, gifts he'd given her for special occasions, and sometimes just because. Everything they'd done to make it theirs was laid out before her life a 3D photo album, and for a moment she was so lost in the memories that she couldn't remember why she was leaving.

Then, as she turned, a twinge of pain tightened the muscles in her neck, and it came back to her at once; the nights she'd laid on the couch with the phone at her side, praying he'd call to say he was okay; the times she'd pleaded with him not to leave and watching him leave anyway; looking in his cloudy, vacant eyes, thinking she'd do anything for him to really see her. She wanted so badly to believe that she was enough for him; that he wouldn't need to drink because she was there. But it was foolish to keep holding onto that, and she knew it. For now, he'd made his choice, and now she had to make one, too.

Taking a deep breath, she opened the door and walked out, leaving her key under the mat.

In the early morning hours Stephen came home and found a letter pinned up by the mirror when he walked in:

Stephen,

I'm sorry, but I need to go away for a while. I need some time for myself right now, and I think it will be good for you, too. We both know there's nothing more that can be done as long as we're together. I can't make you want to change, you have to make the decision for yourself. As much as it hurts, there's nothing left for me to do but tell you goodbye. Hopefully it won't be for good, but that's really up to you. Everything is in your hands.

I'll be at Jess' house for a while, but after that I don't know. Maybe I'll go back home for a while, and see my family. I think it's best if you don't contact me for a little while.

There's some AA pamphlets on the counter for you – Please, take a look at them and consider it. Don't do it for me, do it for yourself.

I love you. Remember that, okay?

-Kate

Nearly six months went by without any word from Stephen. There were times when Kate almost called, or was tempted to drive by to see if he was there, but Jess put a stop to each attempt to contact him. It was for the best, she knew, but it still hurt. A week after she left

Stephen, she quit her job and left school and transferred to a smaller campus nearby, staying away from places she knew he'd come looking for her.

She did go home for a couple weeks, then came back and moved into a house close to Jess. Aside from missing Stephen and wondering how and what he was doing, she was doing pretty well. There was even someone who she was interested in that had asked her out a few times. She didn't feel the same way as when she'd been with Stephen, but she was happy and it felt nice to have someone who cared for her. He was a good man, and she felt safer with him than she had in a long time – but in the back of her mind she always wondered about Stephen and wished he would call.

Then finally one day, she got a letter addressed to her in an unmarked envelope. She took it inside and sat in the recliner, the warm sun on her back. Tearing the envelope open carefully, she took out the paper and read:

Kate,

I'm sorry it's taken me so long to write, but I'm just now finally getting settled. I've missed you – every day, in fact, but I understand why you left and I don't blame you for it. Actually, I'm writing to say thank you. It took losing you for me to decide that I couldn't go on the way I was. You were right; I couldn't do it for you or anyone else, it had to be for me. And I did it.

After you left I went on a three-day drinking binge and was found by a friend passed out in the bathroom. I'm lucky he found me when he did, or I honestly don't know where I'd be right now. Anyway, things were terrible after that; after

The Butterfly Paperweight

I was released from the hospital, I hid out in a hotel room for two weeks – didn't eat, barely slept. I took your letter and some of the booklets you left me, and one day I picked up the phone and called one of the clinics.

Really, I don't know why, but a few days later I was on a plane to Wyoming. I stayed there for two months, and now I'm back home staying at a friend's house until I can get on my feet again. It's still hard, but I haven't touched a thing since I've been out. It doesn't guarantee that I'll never relapse, but one day at a time, you know? And today, I'm doing really well. At least, I feel better than I have in a long time, with the exception of missing you.

With everything I've put you through, I'm not expecting this letter to bring you back, and I've apologized to you so many times that it probably wouldn't mean anything now to say I'm sorry. Whatever you decide to do, I'll understand. But more than anything, I want to tell you I still love you. I didn't always show it the way I should have – or at all, really – but I have always loved you. Hopefully we'll see each other again someday, and I can prove it to you like I should have from the beginning. I'll be waiting for that day. But until then, take care of yourself. I really hope you're well and happy.

Thank you for everything you've done. I could never tell you how much I appreciate it.

Love you always,
Stephen

Kate stared down at the page in her hand, her eyes misty with tears. On the bottom in small print, he'd written the phone number of the place he was staying.

Outside, her boyfriend's car pull up to the curb. She slipped the envelope into her back pocket and wiped away the tears. Two more weeks, she decided, she'd give him two more weeks, and then she'd call. Whatever happened from there would happen on its own. But one thing was certain, there would be no more time wasted for either of them.

Craving

Ten minutes had gone by since Kate pulled into the lot next to the restaurant, parked in the back and shut off the engine. A solid ten minutes and twenty-eight seconds, yet she could not make herself open the car door and get out. She tried, but as she reached for the handle an overwhelming sense of panic stole over her body and forced her to close it again. Closing her eyes as she rested back against on the seat, she exhaled deeply. She clutched the steering wheel as if she were clinging to a life-raft, her only chance for survival in stormy waters. Her knuckles were pure white. It was an improvement, she told herself, from the uncontrollable trembling she experienced just a short while ago as she got ready to leave.

Her mind was like an electrical wire knocked down in a windstorm, writhing madly and spewing sparks. Outwardly however, it looked as if the power line was lying dormant on the ground with all its energy fully expended. It was a strange thing to be internally alive with emotion while showing none of it. She was frozen in place by fear. *Childish, that's exactly how she felt right now, like an eight year old girl in the body of a twenty-one year old woman.* Her car was the reassuringly bright hallway, just enough distance from where the monster lay waiting. Instead of being in bed she was outside an Italian eatery.. It was the kind of place with slightly overpriced food and décor that would only look authentically European to the inexpert eyes of urban American consumers.

It was a nice evening in the city, a romantic night with a clear sky blanketed in stars and a half moon that shone like a pendant suspended on an invisible chain. The unusually-warm-for-February breeze carried with it the promise of spring. The night had all the qualities of a fairytale ending to Valentine's Day

According to her clock quarter until nine o'clock. In fifteen minutes it would be the one-year anniversary of what should have been the cheerful night of her life; the night when her boyfriend, Stephen, had finally proposed. But instead of breaking open a bottle of champagne and celebrating their engagement with friends, Kate's night was spent breaking up a tussle her new fiancé instigated after demolishing the contents of the mini-bar at their friend's party. Afterwards she stood outside and persuaded the police not to haul Stephen off to the county jail so she could take him to get his deviated septum and fractured wrist checked out at the emergency room. Meanwhile she borrowed a friend's scarf to cover her rapidly bruising cheek where she'd intercepted a punch during the fight between two men twice her size that she thought she could referee.

Sitting in the hospital while a doctor who looked at her distrustfully as she explained (lied about) the situation fixed Stephen's nose and fit his arm in a sling, Kate stared down at the half-carat diamond on her finger glistening in the glow of the florescent light. As she brushed the wetness from her cheeks she felt the nauseating stir of realization in her stomach:

You can't marry him, Kate.

Jess took her in for the night and in the morning she drove over to the apartment where she and Stephen lived together and gave him back the ring. He was too drunk to do anything but stare at her vacantly. Two weeks later, she moved out and left him for good. Or at least that's what she intended to do until she received an unexpected letter in the mail.

She adjusted the rear-view mirror and scrutinized her reflection once more; thankfully, all her stress and worry had been mostly concealed by a thin layer – okay, maybe two moderately heavy layers – of foundation and blush. Enough frizz-control shampoo along with a handful of hair product had calmed her usually disarrayed hair, but she raked her fingers through the flaxen curls just to be certain it was perfect. After she was somewhat pleased with her face she fixed the strap of her sky blue dress.

You should have gone with the pink strapless, this lipstick is too red, and could you have put on any more eyeliner? You look like a very tired raccoon. Whose bright idea was it to wear three-inch heels after you've worn nothing but flats in the past six months? Her mind threw every insult at her in rapid-fire succession, cleverly skirting around the actual reason she couldn't step foot outside the car – it was *fear*.

Not that it was a foreign emotion to Kate, since being Stephen Braithwaite's girlfriend meant constantly living in terror -- waiting up by the phone on the brink of a panic attack, hoping it would ring and that it wouldn't at the same time. She was afraid when he didn't come home on

Friday evening after work and even more scared when he did. Stephen's temper could flare any time for any reason, so for a year she walked on eggshells to avoid getting in his line of fire. Near the end of their relationship she avoided going out with him because trouble seemed to follow wherever he went. For an entire twelve months anxiety and worry almost became her natural state of being, so it was no surprise that it had returned with him.

In the process of removing her belongings from Stephen's apartment and breaking all her ties from him, she soon discovered that eliminating her emotional attachment to him would be much more complicated. After she wrote her goodbye letter to Stephen and moved in with Jess' she assumed the worst of it was over, however she quickly began to understand that it was only the tip of the iceberg. Not long after she cut off all contact from him, the emotional trauma he'd inflicted on her began to show; besides refusing to give out her real name in paranoia that it would somehow get back to Stephen, Kate barely left the house except to go to class or work.

Insomnia gradually started taking effect. In the middle of the night she would awake suddenly, her breath hitched in her throat as her heart drummed riotously against her ribcage. Beads of sweat trickled down her face like rain droplets. She lay there bathed in moonlight with silence unbearably close around her, trying to calm herself back to sleep. These episodes became increasingly frequent and intense until finally Kate simply gave up for the fact that sleeping required far more energy than staying up.

Jess was getting tired of watching as her friend became a shell of her former self. She turned to the assistance of Kate's mother in staging an intervention.

The Butterfly Paperweight

Kate's mother drove to Jess' place under the pretense that it was to be a girls' weekend, to help Kate relax. On Sunday as the women sat in the kitchen Jess finally got up the nerve to speak.

"Kate," Jess began, fiddling nervously with the string on her teabag. "There's something your mom and I want to talk to you about." She glanced over at Kate's mother who remained silent.

Kate looked up at her.

"Well, there's someone in the city – a man, his name is Dr. Spindler, who specializes in what you are going through," the words tumbled from Jess' mouth in a continuous string followed by a deep sigh.

Kate blinked.

"It's just one appointment, honey," her mother interposed. "Just so he can get to know you better and you can learn a little more about him. Then, if it's not a good match, you don't have to go back. You don't have to decide anything right away."

Kate still didn't answer. She'd *known* since the day she overheard Jess talking with someone from the phone in the den, and then when her mother called to say that she was coming down to spend a few days with her. All weekend she *knew* this was coming and done everything in her power to avoid it. Now that everything she'd been suspecting was finally out she couldn't believe it. Her most trusted companion and, worse, her *mother* thought she was going crazy.

Looking back and forth between the two, hoping to find just a scrap of compassion in one pair of eyes but finding none, she began to cry. "No, no," she whispered so quietly it almost couldn't be heard. Finding her voice, she spoke more boldly. "No, I won't do it. Don't treat me like I'm a psycho that needs to be taken and locked up somewhere."

"That's not at all what I'm saying, Kate," Jess reasoned, giving Kate's hand a squeeze. "No one is accusing you of being crazy, but you *are* sick. Anyone in your position would have trouble coping. That's why there are people out there who can help you start to figure things out and get your life back together. It's nothing to be ashamed of, there's nothing wrong in admitting you can't do it alone."

"Simple as that, is it, Jess? Pick up the pieces and just move on," Kate said frigidly. "Well, I'm glad that you and this white-coat idiot already have everything figured out. I'm sorry if I'm not up to speed with the rest of you. You know, maybe if I was sitting here and smiling and telling you that everything was okay this wouldn't have come up." Kate was on her feet, towering over them like some angry volcanic goddess in a Greek myth that is about to squelch her victims.

"Katie –" her mother started, reaching out for her daughter once more.

Kate recoiled from her mother's grasp, backing up toward the back door. "Don't touch me, mother." she said in a low, spiteful tone which didn't sound like her even to Kate's ears. "Life is enough of a mess already without you two meddling in my business. Tell your doctor I said to shove his advice, I don't need his brand of help or yours. I'm leaving now, so you don't have to worry about seeing me anymore."

"Kate, will you listen to us, please?" Jess begged, starting after Kate.

The Butterfly Paperweight

She stormed out, the patio door slammed loudly behind her as she left. Kate bolted off in a dead sprint with her mother and Jess calling behind her.

Behind Jess' house there was a small park that Kate and Stephen frequented when the family was out of town. At least once a day they would make up a picnic lunch and hike the long, winding trail until the trees began to diminish until they stopped completely near the small bank of a secluded body of water. Being this far away from the bustling commotion of city life felt like getting transported to an entirely different world. It was so quiet and still that when a bird flew overhead the beating sound of its wings was almost deafening. They would sit talking by the calm, lapping water for an hour or more and even that wasn't enough for Kate. It brought her a sense of peace, and that's what she needed more than ever. She was running so fast that she almost wasn't able to stop once she reached the water, nearly tumbling in. She caught herself and then collapsed, sobbing into her hands.

She couldn't believe what they were doing to her, bringing her so much pain on top of everything while pretending to do her some great service. What good could it do to go to a doctor who didn't really care? There was not a single thing he could tell her that she hadn't already figured out a long time ago – she was a fool who fell for an alcoholic and tolerated – no, not just tolerated, *enabled* – his lying, manipulative, abusive ways because her blind love for him overrode her sensibility. Really, that's all it came down to; despite knowing that it was completely wrong, Kate was still desperately in love.

If for no other reason, she wouldn't go because she would be humiliated. Jess and her mother had been right about that, at least. She was nothing if not proud.

Although she vehemently resisted, ultimately Kate surrendered and drove into the city with Jess on May 12th to see Dr. Spindler. She had never felt more awkward than she did as she sat next to Jess on the uncomfortable waiting room chairs before the doctor, a tall man with silver hair in glasses, called her into his office. When she rose to meet him, he smiled kindly and shook her hand.

"Hello, Kate, I'm Dr. Keith Spindler. How are you doing?

"Fine, I guess."

He ushered her into a smaller room with plaques and awards mounted on the walls and one oblong window, then motioned for her to sit. "Make yourself comfortable, Kate."

She didn't like this guy already, it was irritating the way he insisted on patronizingly saying her name after each sentence. This was a horrible idea. Sitting on the couch across from where he sat behind a small, meticulously organized desk, she averted her eyes and began nervously picking her nails.

"Why have you came to see me, Kate?" He asked, consulting the papers on his clipboard.

"My friend and mother think I need it."

"Do *you* think you need it?"

"I – well, I guess I do, yeah…" she admitted with a sigh. "I just left my boyfriend of one year because of his drinking problem, and well…It's been hard, as you can imagine."

The Butterfly Paperweight

"I can," he agreed with a nod as he scribbled on his notepad. "And how have you been coping with this?"

"You mean, how have I *not* been dealing with it?" She corrected with a small laugh. "If I was handling it I wouldn't be here, would I?"

"Are you in love with –"

"Stephen. His name is Stephen Braithwaite."

"Stephen," Dr. Spindler repeated, scribbling again. "Do you still love him?"

"Being with a substance abuser is like dating a vampire," she told him. "After being around them for a while you start to change into them. Ultimately, I'm an addict just like him. So, am I in love with him? Maybe not, but am I just like him in that I'm controlled by need? Absolutely."

It felt strange to be in a room with a virtual stranger who sat there and wrote down everything she said, but despite her previous objections she actually began to see an improvement with each session she had with Dr. Spindler. He was a gentle man who unlike many psychologists she'd come across seemed to genuinely understand what she was going through, and most importantly she trusted him.

It took a while and there were many ups and downs along the way, but steadily Kate began to mend the pieces of her once broken life and finally got back on her feet. She even allowed Jess to set her up with someone who she knew in school, Mark Edwards. They hit it off immediately. Soon after they called their relationship official, Kate stopped going to Dr. Spindler.

The first time Stephen contacted her it was nearly six months after Kate packed up her things and left. In his letter he apologized profusely and went on to say that he still loved her, he hoped they could eventually resolve things to be together again. He claimed to have been in treatment, sober for three weeks since his return from Wyoming. Though he didn't leave a number or address for her correspondence, he added in a P.S. that he would speak to her soon. Kate hid the note from Mark before later showing it to Jess. They sat at the kitchen table and she pulled the envelope from her purse.

"Yeah, so he's sorry, what else is new?" Jess said disdainfully, tossing it down on the table in repulsion.

"I don't know, Jess. He sounds pretty sincere..."

"Oh, Kate, *please* don't start this again," Jess pleaded with her. "He always *sounds* genuine, that's his game. You've got a nice guy in your life – a truly *nice* guy who cares about you, you're on your way to getting a degree in history to become a teacher like you've always wanted, you're *happy* for once. Don't let him waltz back in and mess everything up. You'll just get your heartbroken again, because he doesn't mean a word he says."

Kate sighed heavily. As usual, Jess made a lot of good sense. "I know, you're right, I just needed to hear somebody say it is all. Thanks, Jess."

"Good," Jess said with a relieved smile. She ran the letter through the paper shredder, and then once more just for effect.

Of course Kate did not just forget the letter, but she never mentioned it to Jess or anyone else again. Her relationship with Mark grew and she fell in love with him, although Stephen never fully left her mind. She often wondered how he was doing, if he was living close by and if he was sober. Without any way of getting in touch with him, though, all she could do is wonder and try not to let it bother her – sometimes it worked, sometimes it didn't. He didn't write or call her after that, and eventually life once again got back to normal.

Time has a way of slipping past us before we have a chance to see and capture it. Before she knew summer's warm quietly succumbed to the coolness of autumn, then in a blink Valentine's Day was here. The previous month had been full of excitement and Kate upon return to Michigan, was settling into life as an engaged woman. Mark invited her to join him at his family's reunion in California, and one night as they sat in the middle of his relatives on the beach he knelt down in front of her as he asked her to be his wife. After several minutes Kate finally composed herself and said yes.

Immediately after they got home, Jess insisted they start planning *now* even though Kate and Mark had decided to wait a year before getting married. As she told Kate, "There's no such thing as being overly prepared. In case anything changes, you need a plan."

Little did she know how prophetic her words actually were. The week of Valentines day she received another letter from Stephen. This time he said that it was imperative that he speak with her and if possible see her again. He included a phone number and implored her to call him as soon as she could. Once again he signed off by saying that he loved her.

Kate didn't go to Jess for counsel again – she already knew what had to be done. Before she left she called Mark in from the living room and sat next to him on the stools by the counter.

"Do you remember my ex-boyfriend Stephen? I've told you about him before," she began, making her speech up as she went along.

"Yes," he said with a worried frown, his eyes widened in horror. "What's he done now, Katie? Is he after you again, did he try to hurt you?"

Katie, she hated to be called that. Stephen never used that nickname with her. "No, it's nothing like that. He just wants to meet up and talk."

"Well, you're not going. You *can't* go," he exclaimed, but there was an edge of nervous uncertainty in his voice. "Katie, how do you know he's not going to do something when you get there? What if he's been drinking again?"

"He doesn't drink anymore."

"So he claims," Mark retorted, the aggravation in his voice now coming through loud and clear. "He can say whatever he wants, but he's *lying*, Katie, he always lies to you. You can't go."

Kate grimaced inwardly. Suddenly, Mark sounded exactly like Jess had on the day she approached her about therapy; condescending, like she was too stupid to make the right decision on her own. "I have to go, Mark, we're meeting in an hour. This is something I need to do, for myself, if only to gain some closure."

He opened his mouth to protest, but she stood up and walked out the door before the argument could go on. She'd listened and followed the advice of everyone around her, but now she was doing what *she* knew was right. It was the only way she could ever truly heal.

Fear had not been a part of her life for several months now, but now it settled inside of her chest and burned her stomach. It felt like seeing an old friend after ten or more years apart; uncomfortable, but familiar.

One last thing about fear occurred to her; to conquer it, you have to grit your teeth face it head-on. The little boy will never feel safe in his bed until he goes in one night with a flashlight and inspects under his bed, seeing for himself that a monster is not waiting to snatch him up and eat him alive. Breaking up with Stephen had been her worst imaginable nightmare until she had no choice but to do it. Therapy had seemed horrifying before she actually went to speak with a psychologist, Dr. Spindler.

Kate opened the door and stepped onto the asphalt. The moon was higher, radiantly bright in the endless black. Lukewarm night air swept around her in gentle drafts, making her dress swish lightly around her legs. It felt like there was too much air out here in contrast to her tight-spaced car, as if her lungs were filling up too rapidly and she would soon drown in oxygen.

As Kate entered the restaurant a young couple exited, their hands clasped as they walked close together. On the young, doe-eyed girl's left hand a new, burnished diamond twinkled in the light. She gave Kate a hazily blissful smile that Kate tried but failed to match.

She quickly surveyed the room with her eyes, but could not find Stephen. Maybe he wasn't there yet. She walked over to the matri 'd and waited for his attention.

"Excuse me," she asked quietly. "I'm meeting someone, but I'm not sure if he's arrived yet."

" Kate Ackerly? Mr. Braithwaite came in half an hour ago, he requested that I see you to his table," the man informed her, walking around his desk and motioning Kate to come with him.

She nodded and followed him silently. He led her back to a table in front of a window that offered a luxurious view of the city skyline. Stephen was sitting there, looking off into the distance and sipping a glass of water. He turned when he heard them walk over.

Kate politely waved the matri d' away with a thank you, then stood there and looked at Stephen. He got to his feet and came toward her.

"Hi, Kate," he said quietly, holding open his arms to embrace her.

"Hi," she answered with a forced smile. Her stomach jumped and flipped around, twisting into a thousand knots. She suddenly felt as if she had taken a leap off the edge of a cliff and was now free-falling down into a deep ravine where she didn't know if she'd be met by soft ground or a bed of jagged boulders.

They held onto each other for a long moment, and despite the madness of her emotions being in his arms was like being at home. She turned her face into his neck, finding there was not a single trace of alcohol on him. Squeezing him once more before letting go, she gazed up at him with great affection. Odd as it was to her she realized that before now she'd never taken notice of how astoundingly blue his eyes were, cobalt with flecks of green. Excessive drinking had faded their intensity, but now they were clear and bright and stunning.

"Thank you for coming," he told her. "It's so good to see you again."

"It's good to see you, too, Steve. You look…great," she replied as they sat down.

"You do, too, but that's not surprising. How are you doing?"

"I'm great…well, you know, I've been well," she added with a laugh. "I'm still going to school, about to graduate this summer. And I'm substituting history at a grade school after that until I get a permanent teaching job, hopefully at the high school across town." She paused briefly, looking down into the glass of water that had been placed in front of her. "And I met someone a few months ago. We're getting married next year."

She half-expected him to explode in a jealous rage and come across the table at her. But his eyes only darkened momentarily before he grinned broadly. "Well, again I can't say I'm surprised, I figured it wouldn't be long before some lucky guy snatched you up. What's his name?"

"Mark Hammond."

"Is he good to you?" Stephen asked.

"He's very good to me," she confirmed.

"After being with me I guess anyone is an improvement…" he muttered, staring down at his hands. He cleared his throat, straightening up in his chair. "I'm happy for you. Really, I honestly am, babe. Like I told you in my letter, you deserve happiness and I'm just sorry I wasn't the one to give it to you."

She fought against the sudden rush of tears that swelled in her eyes and reached over to put her hand on top of his. He squeezed back tenderly and smiled.

"Why did you want to see me?" She asked, even though she wasn't sure whether she really wanted to hear the reason or not.

"I wanted to apologize to your face, sending a letter didn't seem like enough. I wanted to say how sorry I am and that I never meant for us to end up this way."

"It's okay, Steve –"

"No, please, let me finish. When you and I first met I was a complete mess, no one knows that more than you. Becoming a product of your environment is a sorry excuse, but there were so many things in my past that I wanted to forget, like my father dying when I was seven and my mother being all but absent except when she'd bring one of her boyfriends home and let them do whatever they wanted to me and my sisters. No matter what I did I could never get past it."

"That's when you came into my life. You were the most amazing thing that ever happen to me and I – I got scared, if you can believe that. It didn't seem possible that someone like you would have wanted to be anywhere near me, let alone actually want to be *with* me. Everyone that I'd met before had given up on me, I figured after a while you would, too, but then you *stayed*," he explained, and Kate almost swore there were tears in his eyes. "I couldn't believe it, and soon my disbelief turned into resentment. Because I know what you've been through even before me, but you didn't let it ruin you the way it did me. You were *okay* and I didn't know why I couldn't be like you."

"I'm not perfect, Steve," she informed him, leaning in close to him over the table. "I'm nowhere close to perfect."

"Well, you're a better actor," he said with attempted humor, but his voice cracked as he spoke and he ducked out of the light to wipe his eyes. "People who have gotten hurt in their lives end up hurting other people. I was so lost in my own pain that I hurt the one person I never intended to hurt and I had to ask your forgiveness. I needed to say it because you deserve to hear it, and I need to hear you."

"I could never be angry with you even after I left – I wanted to be, but I couldn't be. I wasn't angry because I *understood* what you were going through. All my life I'd been told I wasn't good enough, whether it was my mother telling me to do better in school, or the guys I went to school with that rejected me. Until you came along I'd convinced myself that I was unlovable and no one could ever want me," she spoke quietly, running her thumb across his knuckles. "I don't think a person could get any lower than when they deem themselves unworthy of love, and when you're at that point you'll grab onto anything that might prove you wrong even if it's not healthy. Our relationship became a security blanket for me. You and I are exactly the same, we just chose a different kryptonite; yours was alcohol, mine was you."

He smiled and nodded. "Will you forgive me?"

She smiled back. "Of course, you're absolutely forgiven."

"Well then...To forgiveness?" He asked as he raised his glass.

"To recovery and no longer being dependant," she corrected while tapping her glass lightly against his. She leaned back and studied him closely. "How long have you been sober?"

"Oh, I almost forgot," he mumbled as he took his wallet from his pocket and fished out a small gold coin, handing it to her. It was an AA coin that read "To Thine Own Self Be True" with the serenity prayer on the opposite side. "I got it today because I'm nearing the end of my program and I've not had a drink in almost a year."

She held it out in front of her with her thumb and forefinger. "That's great, congratulations!"

"Thanks. I want you to have it."

"What?" She asked incredulously. "No way, Steve, it's yours and you've *earned* it. No, I can't take it."

"No, Kate, it really belongs to you," he told her. "You're the reason I decided to go into treatment in the first place, I never would have done it had it not been for you."

She looked down at it uncertainly, but couldn't help the swell of pride she felt. "I still think you should have it, but if it's what you really want —"

"It is," he told her with firm certainty.

Before she knew it they were back at her place and it was past 1:00 in the morning. Earlier she narrowly avoided a kiss, but as they were saying goodbye he pecked her lips gently and she couldn't resist. Against her better judgment she asked him to come home with her. Now she fumbled with the front door lock as they stood on her porch, and then started to pull him inside. He stopped in the doorway hesitatingly.

"What?" She asked with a puzzled frown.

"You know there's nothing I want more than to stay with you," he said, tucking a piece of her hair behind her ear.

"But *what*?" she urged, standing in front of him.

"But, are you sure this isn't some impulsive decision that you're going to regret tomorrow?" He asked, putting his hands on her waist.

She paused to consider it. There was Mark, of course, but he was gone visiting a friend and wouldn't be home until the weekend. No one else would ever find out, and if she let Stephen go she may never see him again. This was her only chance.

Slowly she wrapped her arms around his neck and answered with a kiss.

The next morning Kate awoke before Stephen and laid there in the orange-gold morning light as she watched him sleep. He was facing her with his face partially buried in the pillow. It felt right waking up beside him, and yet there was still the engagement ring on her finger. She wondered if she could ever feel at home like this with Mark, but she didn't want to contemplate the answer. Quietly she rose from his side and got dressed, then grabbed her keys from the nightstand and left to go for a drive. Being with Stephen made her feel even more insecure with her decision to get married to someone else, and now she needed to be alone.

Whenever Kate needed to clear her mind she would go for a drive. Though she never had a destination, but her goal was just to drive as far away as she could from whatever it was that was bothering her. Anywhere she went, most of the time when she returned from one of her aimless excursions the web of tangled worry in her mind was untied and disposed of. Hopefully it would happen today.

Mark's face and the feeling of being with Stephen dueling in her mind. She continued on along the river and then made a turn into the heart of Detroit. Scenes of city life rolled past her as she navigated her car through the busy streets. Quickly she began to realize that driving around the city where she and Stephen used to spend most of their free time was not the best idea, every sight brought forth a memory of something they shared; during the summer they'd gone to several of the annual music festivals held at Hart Plaza, usually ending with them dancing near the illuminated cylindrical fountain. For her birthday he spent every cent he'd earned for two months in order to buy tickets of *The Color Purple*. It suddenly occurred to her that nearly every square inch of downtown had played a part in their relationship. Finally, she turned back toward home.

On her way back home, Kate abruptly veered off the road and pulled up by the curb. At the same time her cell phone beeped twice, alerting her of a text message from Mark.

Hey baby, it read. *I got a late start from Alex's place but I'm on my way home now, do you need anything? I was miserable being separated from you this weekend, Katie, I miss you. Every day I realize how empty and void my life is without you. But soon we'll be married and then we'll never have to spend another day apart, will we? I can't wait. Anyway, see you soon. I love you.*

She threw it down on the passenger seat and hunched over the wheel, sobbing into her arms. Before her life had been fine, *she* was fine, and then her old alcoholic flame decided now was the perfect time for him to put a wedge between her and true happiness once again. And the worst part was now hers were not the only feelings at stake but Mark's as well. The heart of a man was in jeopardy, a *good* man who had been nothing but kind, and generous, and patient with her as she healed. *Damn you,* she cursed him fiercely. *Damn you, Stephen Braithwaite.*

Soon her crying tapered off into silent tears and she calmed herself enough to keep driving. She called Mark to say that she and Jess had decided to go out for the evening, and then drove over to Stephen's.

The Butterfly Paperweight

Three months later, Kate was continually sneaking around with Stephen and finding ways to keep her secret from Jess, her mother, and especially Mark. On weekends she would make up an excuse, usually 'wedding plans' were her cover, and then spend three days with Stephen. He called her frequently at work and they would arrange quick rendezvous during their breaks. Mark worked all week and Stephen would often come over until he was due home in the afternoon. The guilt was crippling, yet not enough for her to say no when Stephen would call and say he was coming over. At the end of the day, the way she felt about Stephen was undeniable and nothing, not even the danger of losing her relationship, was enough to sway her.

One day Kate called Stephen to ask if he wanted to go down by the waterfront. It was a delightfully hot June day and it would be a shame to waste it. Mark wouldn't be home for another five or six hours. Stephen told her that he'd get off work in about forty-five minutes and then he would swing by to get her. Kate was in a good mood today. She wasn't feeling particularly ashamed of anything nor was she bothered that she was once again sneaking out like a rebellious teenager escaping from her bedroom in the middle of the night. She hummed lightly as she made a picnic lunch for two and got dressed in a black tank top paired with a barely-there skirt. While she was in the kitchen making sandwiches, the back door opened and someone came in.

"Hey, Ste," she called, not looking up. "I didn't think you were coming for a while, but I'm almost ready. Just decided that we should have something to eat while we're down at the river…" She paused and frowned at his non-response. "Steve?"

"Guess again, Katie," Jess said flatly as she came into the kitchen.

"Jess," Kate whispered in surprise, her stomach churned. "Um, hi…What are you doing her?"

"You left your cell phone at my house last night," she told her, holding it out to Kate. Her face was calm, but Kate saw the dark cloud of anger brewing in her eyes. She was livid. "No wonder I haven't seen much of you lately, it appears that you're quite the busy girl. In the last fourteen hours you've had three calls, a text message, along with approximately two dozen text messages." She flipped the phone open and began reviewing the text message inbox. "Then again, maybe not since every single one is from the same number."

Kate didn't answer, she just stood there with the butter knife in hand looking as if she had seen a ghost. There was no use coming up with a story, Jess wouldn't have believed it and didn't seem like she was in the mood for games anyway. She was caught red-handed, now all she could do was confess and hope for mercy. "Jess, listen to me, I can explain…" She started, but had no idea where to begin.

"Can you really? Well then, please, by all means. I'd love to hear it," Jess said as she plunked down in a chair with her arms crossed, looking at Kate expectantly.

Kate sat across from her, forcing herself to speak despite her cracking voice. "Steve and I have been seeing each other for three months," she began, staring at her hands to avoid looking at Jess. "Remember the letter I got from him in February asking me out to dinner? I went and we had a long talk, he told me he's been sober for a year. He even gave me this…" She brought the coin out from where she kept it inside her wallet and showed it to Jess. "Jess, you should have seen him that night, he was so sincere and honest with me. That night he stayed with me, and ever since then we've been getting together a few times a week." She finally looked up and met Jess' eyes.

"Has the fact that you're engaged to be married conveniently slipped your mind?" Jess asked, her tone still that of a harsh disciplinarian that was about to dispense the harshest punishment.

"No…" Kate answered sheepishly, her face turning red.

"Oh, so you're just cheating on your fiancé, then?"

"No!" She protested defensively. "No, that's not it, Jess. I would never intentionally hurt Mark. But…this is a complicated situation, you know. What am I supposed to do, just ignore how I feel about Stephen and pretend like the whole situation doesn't exist? It's not that easy."

"No, it takes maturity and integrity to look beyond yourself and take responsibility for your actions, which are two qualities you severely lack," Jess spat furiously, glaring at her friend with daggers in her eyes.

Kate recoiled at her spiteful words. Hurt tears sprung to her eyes.

"It's so easy for you, isn't it, Jess? For you to sit there and judge me is so very easy since you're just *perfect*. You're perfect and I'm the invariable screw-up who just isn't *mature* and *responsible* enough to make the right decision," she riposted venomously. "But you know what? You're *wrong*. For once I am thinking for myself and doing what I want, and my decision is not going to waver just because you or my mother think I shouldn't. And what business is it of yours, anyway? Like you said it's *my* life."

Now both girls were standing at opposite ends of the kitchen table, looking like two cats with their hair standing on end, ready to pounce and claw each other. The coin had fallen off onto the floor and was lying at their feet. Neither of them heard Stephen's car pull up before he came in.

"If you want to ruin your life for that worthless drunk, then be my guest," Jess sneered. "But don't come back crying to me the first time he downs a bottle of vodka and beats you senseless."

"Get *out*," Kate growled back, pointing toward the door.

Jess whipped around without another word and brushed passed Stephen who stood by the door, the door banged shut behind her.

"What—" he started to ask, coming over to Kate.

"I don't want to talk about it," she said. "Let's just go, okay?"

He didn't argue, they packed up their stuff and went down to the river. People milled about the waterfront as boats and ferries passed under the Ambassador Bridge then disappeared from sight. The sun was bright in the clear blue sky, a whisper of a breeze rustled through the trees. Kate and Stephen parked and walked through St. Aubin Park, finding shade under a willow tree by the water. Neither spoke for several minutes.

"Maybe Jess was right –" Stephen began to say.

"No, she wasn't," Kate stopped him abruptly. "She's a control-freak who doesn't know when to stay out of things she doesn't belong in to begin with."

"I don't want you to ruin everything for me, Kate," he told her calmly. "You have someone that loves you who probably has a better history of being dependable than I do. Even with all that at stake are you sure you want to be here right now?"

"I'm sure," Kate told him confidently, she crawled into his lap and kissed him with a smile. "Now I think I said I don't want to talk about it anymore."

Two weeks later Kate stood in a bridal shop with her mother on her left and Jess on her right. Despite their confrontation Kate did not have a replacement maid-of-honor and so Jess was forced to come dress shopping with them. They had been to many different stores, but Kate still hadn't found the dress she was looking for. She looked in the five angled mirrors at the strapless ivory gown and ran her fingers lightly over the ornately beaded bodice. Her mother gushed behind her.

"Oh, Katie, it's perfect!" she exclaimed. "You look absolutely gorgeous. Jess, isn't she stunning?"

"Unbelievable," Jess agreed with a forced smile. Kate gave her a look in the mirror.

"What do you think, honey?" Kate's mother asked. "Do you like it?"

"Yeah, I do," Kate said thoughtfully, examining her reflection. "I do, mom, but there were some others I liked, too. Maybe I just need to think it over."

"Indecisiveness has always been your nature," Jess remarked dryly. Kate shot her another hard look.

Kate's mother didn't notice Jess' quip. "Of course, dear, you don't have to decide anything today. We still have plenty time."

She got off the pedestal and went back to the fitting room to change. Afterwards she told her mother that she needed to be getting back home, diverting the suggestion they go to another store. Before her mother could say much of anything Kate pecked her on the cheek and sped out. As she left she could hear Jess comment on how busy Kate was.

Kate drove around for a while before she went home. Mark was sitting on the couch with his feet propped up on the coffee table, reading. He looked up when Kate came in.

"Hey," she said as she sat down beside him.

"Hey, babe," he leaned over to kiss her forehead. "How did the Great Dress Hunt go?"

"Oh, you know, like all shopping excursions with my mother go," she said. She touched her diamond ring. "Mark, there's something I have to tell you."

He marked his page and set the book aside, looking at her. "All right, shoot."

"Mark, I love you. You're the nicest, smartest, most kind-hearted person I know," she began. "You are the kind of guy most girls I know would kill to date. But..." she paused and slipped off the ring, holding it between her fingers. "But I'm not *in love* with you."

Mark's face turned white. "*What?*"

"When I first met you I was just starting to get my life back in order and I wanted so desperately to find someone who could prove to me that I wasn't doomed to walk the world completely alone," she said. "But all the while I wasn't falling in love with *you*, I was falling in love with everything you *weren't* – you're nothing like Stephen, and I thought someone like you is exactly what I needed. The problem is, I'm in love with Stephen."

He fell silent for a moment as she put the ring in his hand, and then he sighed deeply. "You know, I always thought you were."

"You did?" She asked, unbelieving.

"Whenever I'm with you it's like you're here but you're not with me. There's a piece of you missing, that part will always belong to him. I knew from the beginning that you didn't love me, but you were trying to get away from the life you'd had before. I did the same thing. I wanted a wife, someone to settle down with, but it wasn't you."

"I guess we both thought by marrying each other we could erase the past," she said.

"The past can't be erased, only learned from. And in the end, you have learned something; that you need to follow your heart," he smiled a little. "So go and follow it."

She smiled and leaned up to kiss him. "Thank you."

He smiled back and watched her go, still holding the ring in his palm.

Kate wasn't sure if she was right or wrong, but ultimately she discovered it really didn't matter to her. Life is all about choices, and in the end how it all turns out cannot be foreseen. All we can do is be true to ourselves and follow the path that will ultimately lead us wherever we're supposed to go. Every now and then our road travels back to somewhere we've been before to bring us to our future. Kate's path had led back to

Stephen, and no matter where it went she knew she'd follow it to the end.

All for Love

There is no greater power

Than that of love.

It is for love the earth we scour.

We search here, below, even above

That unshakable force

Of which we have no control.

One moment when we allow nature to take its course,

We give away our hearts, even our souls.

Everything is compromised: our dreams, our aspirations, and goals.

Because love is what truly makes us whole.

Everything would be given away

For the gift of love, losing everything is worth.

For love, I will forever scour the earth.

Going Back

The sign ahead read: NEW HAVEN-NEXT LEFT. Jimmy flipped on his blinker, before merging into the north-bound lane. The low rumbling of the traffic on the interstate highway hummed outside the window, tiny drops of rain pattered softly against the windows. Usually when he drove, especially on long trips such as this one, he would have been accompanied by Bob Dylan or The Who, but not today. Today he had too much to think about.

The early morning sky had awoken in a bright, vibrant shade of blue, but as he moved closer to his hometown it had flattened to a dull slate-gray. He didn't notice the change, and it was almost subconsciously that he had turned on his windshield wipers as the first droplets of rain began to fall. In fact, from the time he reached the highway and began westward he had been driving on autopilot; every turn and lane-change purely instinctual. His eyes stared, dark and pensive, at the endless stretch of black road.

Finally, the white sign with the large black letters that declared: YOU ARE NOW ENTERING NEW HAVEN came into view.

"Home, sweet home," he murmured to himself, barely aware he had spoken aloud.

He descended down the off-ramp that led down to the first four-way stop in town. It was just past 3:15, so he had just managed to miss the 4:00 rush-hour when school let out and people started to get off work.

A sweeping nostalgia washed over him as he passed between the Willow Branch Apartment complex and gas station at the edge of town. It hardly resembled the place he had spent the first twenty-one years of his life in; the town square of antique shops, bakeries, and family owned restaurants had been replaced by a modernized strip mall of fast food chains, swanky clothes boutiques, and corporate banks. Olson's Food & Drug was now replaced by a Safeway supermarket. A pang of sadness ran through him.

Olson's was run by an elderly couple, Ernest and Cecilia. Mr. Olson was a thin, frail-looking man who stood at a mere five-foot-four. Despite the fact that he came to America with his family when he was only eight-years-old, his German accent was still quite evident bushy, black eyebrows drooped above his deep-set chocolate eyes. His cheeks were sunken in with age and time, and were always a blazing, feverish red on his high cheekbones. A mustache curled across his thin upper-lip, always neatly trimmed. Not-so-neatly trimmed was his hair; Mrs. Olson had been cutting it herself for the past fifty-two years, and due to her increasingly bad eyesight and shaky hands, his bangs always fell on his forehead in an uneven slant like fringe on a lamp-shade in his grandmother's house. Mr. Olson's love and affection for his wife kept him from ever complaining about it, and he always managed to seem eager when time came for another trim.

Cecilia was a robust Italian woman who was considerably taller and much sturdier than her husband. She wore brightly colored, flowered dresses which she had designed herself, the hem of each one matched Mr. Olson's uneven hair. Her white hair was always pulled back in a tight bun and fastened by a silver butterfly clip. She wore too much rouge and painted her hazel eyes with powder blue eye shadow which flaked into her long eyelashes. She was in every way the typical Italian woman, running the bakery in the store and always insisting that you take a cinnamon roll or Danish on your way out. Her voice was almost more masculine than her husband, and she was brazenly loud with a hearty laugh. If she was irritated enough she would grab a broom from the storage closet and chase after them, waving it furiously in front of her and yelling in Italian. Despite her tough exterior, she was a warm, loving woman who was devoted to 'Her Ernie' and treated every one as if they were her own.

From the time he was old enough for his mother to let him walk there by himself, every Tuesday he made a trip to Olson's to pick up groceries for the week. On each visit, Olson would slip him two Tootsie Rolls and a cream soda. Jimmy would boost himself up on one of the stools at the long, white marble counter, his legs swinging six or more inches above the black-and-white tiled floor. He waited in anticipation as Mr. Olson took a tall, wide-mouthed glass from the stack on the back counter, took it over to the fountain and pulled the handle of the tap up with a quick jerk of his wrist. The soda flowed out of the nozzle in an amber-colored waterfall, foaming and bubbling as it filled the glass. Just before the glass looked in danger of overflowing, Mr. Olson snapped the tap back up and set the glass next to Jimmy's arm. His hand fumbled around in his apron as he pulled out the two Tootsie Rolls and laid them next to the soda.

"Now remember," he warned kindly, his eyes glinting beneath his eyebrows. "Don't tell your mother." He gave Jimmy a sly wink and a playful smile.

"I won't!" Jimmy promised. Mr. Olson dropped a red straw into the glass and Jimmy began to drink excitedly. Sometimes if the store was particularly quiet, Mr. Olson would make himself a root beer float and bring over the canister of red licorice ropes from near the candy rack, then sit next to Jimmy and tell him stories of when he was in the army. Jimmy stared up at him in fascination, listening intently at every word.

"Ernie!" Mrs. Olson would scold as she came over from behind the cash register, her hands on her wide hips. "You're scaring him! He's going to have nightmares for weeks!"

"Oh, hush up, woman. I'm in the middle of a story," he would say in annoyance, waving a hand at her.

"Ernest Arnold Olson!" She enunciated each word, narrowing her eyes at him.

"Sorry, dear..." He mumbled quietly, staring down into his root beer.

"That's better," she said, smiling in satisfaction.

He furrowed his brow, but then sighed in resignation and closed the canister before he stood up. "I suppose she's right, I should let you get home." He glanced toward the door to make sure his wife wasn't within earshot, and then winked at Jimmy again, "Come see me later, then I'll finish the story."

Jimmy would smile and nod agreeably, although he wished he could sit and listen to Mr. Olson all day.
He watched as Mr. Olson put the licorice back in place, finished off his float, washed and restacked the glass, then went back to work.

After the last drop of cream soda had been coaxed from the bottom of the glass, Mr. Olson gave Jimmy the groceries and medication, and Jimmy dropped two dollars into the old man's hand.

"There you are, my boy," Mr. Olson said, smiling warmly down at the little boy.

"Thanks, Mr. Olson!" Jimmy grinned back at him. He gathered the bags up in his hand and headed for the door. Just then, Mrs. Olson came out of the kitchen carrying a tray of warm sticky buns and raspberry filled doughnuts.

"We'll see you again soon, Jimmy!" She called after him. "Tell your mother I said hello!"

He walked out into the cool afternoon air, heading down Main Street and then up the hill to Willow Road. As he walked he peeled the wrapper off one of the candies and put it in his mouth, then slipped the other into the back pocket of his jeans.

Now he had to physically shake the memory from his mind and realized he had been smiling. In his mind he could still smell the medicinal scent that came from the pharmacy, mixed with lemony Lysol and the sweet aroma of Mrs. Olson's baking. He loved them both. Come to think of it, Mr. Olson was the closest thing Jimmy had ever had to a real father. Even after he left, he had sent them a Christmas card to them every single year, but last year it came back with a 'Return To Sender' stamp. He figured they had probably finally retired and moved.

The Butterfly Paperweight

A few blocks away, the library had also fallen into the clutches of the beast that was reconstruction. The once conservatively tall, two-story dark brick building was now sleek and white, and stretched out from where the original structure had stood to the edge of Kasack Way where the out post-office had been.

He remembered on Fridays after school he would walk down to the post office to drop off his mother's bills, and then walk over to the library. Aubrey Lassana, the raven-haired nineteen-year-old that lived across the street worked at the information desk on weekends, and Jimmy would sit in the chairs by the Science Fiction section, pretending to read and watching her. She was the prettiest girl he had ever seen, and in his nine-year-old heart he was in love with her, the low-cut tops and denim skirts she wore. Every now and then she would walk his way to re-stack a book, as she passed she gave him a radiant smile, her hair falling around the curves of her face in soft waves. He quickly averted his eyes, frantically reading the same sentence over and over, his cheeks flaming red.

He laughed quietly to himself. Three weeks before school let out for the summer, he overheard his mother talking to his aunt.

"Did you hear the news? Aubrey Davis and David Witcham are getting married this summer. He found a job in Tennessee, they'll be moving there after the wedding."

That night, Jimmy was barely able to eat dinner, and for weeks after that he avoided the library like the plague.

Finally, he turned down Cobalt Road towards the elementary school. The playground stood empty, cast in dreary bluish-gray light; a graveyard of his childhood, a graveyard filled with phantoms. One of them was him, a seven-year-old fair-haired boy with his eyes tightly shut and his arms stretched out as he walked across the top of the monkey bars. His sister had demonstrated how easy it was, and not to be outdone, he took her challenged when she dared him to do it.

"I bet you won't," she goaded, her eyes glinting in the high-noon sun.

"Will too," he said with defiant ferocity, then turned and walked valiantly toward the monkey bars.

The entire third and fourth grade crowded around the jungle gym, watching with grim faces as if he were Evel Knievel attempting to jump across the Grand Canyon with no safety gear. He took his time climbing to the top, and then slowly brought himself to a standing position between the first and second rungs. The ground below swelled then receded beneath him like in the Road Runner cartoons he watched every Saturday when the Coyote chased him to the edge of a cliff and Road Runner found himself staring down a seventy-five foot drop, inches away from plummeting to his death.

His courage wavered and he crouched down to his knees, grabbing onto the sidebars, his heart pounding in his ears. For a moment he considered backing down. After all, enduring taunts from his sister and classmates couldn't be worse than breaking his neck, could it? He thought so until he opened his eyes and saw his sister, front and center in the crowd, her arms crossed over her chest expectantly and a knowing smile on her face. He let out his breath; it billowed out in a white cloud like a thought bubble in a comic strip. Steadily, he stood upright again and spread his arms out, closing his eyes. He stepped carefully on the first four rungs, then as his confidence heightened, his pace quickened. Almost sure he was near the end; he stuck his foot out expecting to the last bar to descend the ladder to the bottom. However, in reality he was little more than halfway across, and overstepping caused his heel to slip against the next bar. He tumbled forward, the bars slamming into his groin as he fell. It felt as if someone had driven a screwdriver into his left thigh. Frantically he tried to grab onto the sidebar to catch himself, but his hand slipped and he was left hanging there with his legs twisted around the bars and his upper body dangling. The ground swelled and receded again. He was stuck. Finally, he wriggled his left leg free and went plummeting to the ground with a sickening thud.

Jimmy landed on his stomach, the full force of his bodyweight slammed down on his arm. A red-hot pain exploded from the wrist to the elbow, as if someone had lit an M-80 and set it off inside his arm. The bark dust scratched at his face, leaving tiny splinters in his cheeks and eyelids. Warm, salty blood flooded his mouth, and he realized he had bitten through his tongue. His bottom lip was swollen and throbbing. He began to spit, and blood-soaked clumps of bark dust flew out of his mouth. Mrs. Klaussan's shrieking, panicked voice came from somewhere above.

"Jimmy Oversteen! What do you think you're doing?! You other kids, get back to class! Go on, get!" Her rough, strong hands were on his shoulders then, turning him over on his back. The drilling pain shot through his groin again and his arm screamed, protesting the sudden movement. He continued to spit blood and splinters.

The next minute he was sitting on the bed in the nurse's office as she immobilized his arm, his mother standing over him, crying and asking him what he was thinking over and over. His sister stood in the corner of the room, her face pale with horror. He spent the next week with his arm in a cast and a shiner.

He flexed his hand as a twinge runs down to his elbow, the kind of aching pain that you feel when you dream you break your arm, then awake to find it asleep and tingling; a phantom pain.

At last, his mother's house came into view. He turned left and pulled into the driveway, shutting off his engine. The house was exactly as it was when he was twenty. A cream and black trim, two-story, gable-faced house with sunburst wooden décor and triple multi-pane fixed sash. The shallow bay on the second floor had two double-hung multi-pane windows with an arched center section. The first floor had a bay window with a center single-hung window with art glass transom. A porch swing still sat by the door, swaying lightly in the wind as if some unseen person was sitting there, rocking back and forth. Even the basketball hoop he got for Christmas when he was fourteen was still hanging above the garage. It was as if someone had pasted an old photograph in the middle of a computerized, state-of-the-art 3D model; it seemed completely out of place, yet a warm sense of comfort washed over him as soon as he saw it.

As he began to climb out of the car, a voice came from the porch. "Jimmy?"

He knew it was his mother. She came down the steps and walked toward him hesitantly, as if she wasn't sure if he was actually her son. She was wider in the hips than he remembered; her blue dress seemed too snug around her midsection. As she came closer he saw her hair, drawn up in a bun, was almost completely silver. It had been fifteen years since he had been home, but he felt as if he were looking at a woman who had aged an extra twenty-five; though she seemed grateful to see him, her eyes looked at him with a tired dreariness of someone who has seen everything twice over in her lifetime, the deep lines in her face a testament to each of her long, hard years. She stopped in front of him, studying him closely.

After a moment, he smiled. "Hi, mom."

She grinned, her thin lips stretched out across her tight skin, the crows-feet around her eyes crinkling. Then she was hugging him then, squeezing him tightly. He wrapped his arms around her, hugging her just as tight. When they stepped back again he saw her eyes were misty with tears. She held him by the shoulders.

"Welcome home."

"Thanks," he said, and kissed her cheek. A few awkward moments passed before he finally got his things from the trunk and followed her wordlessly inside.

The inside was unchanged as well. Jimmy felt as if he had stepped through a time portal and reappeared in the world of his childhood. Smells of roasting chicken and baking bread rushed toward him, mixing in with the slightly musty scents of time and age. A large poinsettia in a green, hand-made pot stood between the entryway and the living room. The same wallpaper of vertical green stripes and sunflowers covered the walls between the baseboards. A chair, loveseat, and couch set formed a semi-circle around the deep mahogany coffee table which his grandfather had given his mother as a wedding present, all in the same white polyester slip-covers with blooming, dusty pink roses. The grandfather clock stood in the corner near the fireplace, the gold pendulum swinging back and forth.

His mother began to slip his jacket off his shoulders. "Here, take this off, relax for a while. I made your favorite dinner. Your room is all set up upstairs…"

He nodded, hearing but not really listening. Her voice droned in the background as if coming from the end of a long tunnel in a dream. He surveyed his childhood home, taking in every smell and sight. His eyes settled on the banister leading up the staircase to the second floor. A new memory flooded in; he and his sister, 9 and 11, left alone in the new house after school. *Their mother worked two jobs, so she usually got home around dinnertime on weekdays. They decided it was time to 'break in' the new staircase, and had gone down into the basement to retrieve the unpacked boxes and their mother's laundry basket. Once they were upstairs, they struggled to get themselves into the boxes. They decided they were never going to fit together, so one at a time they crawled inside while the other pushed the box or basket, while the other gave them a good, hard shove. The box tumbled down the stairs to the first landing, crashing into the wall. The pusher would chase after it, reposition it, and send it flying to the bottom. The one who was inside the box would then crawl out, dizzy and giggling hysterically, and they would run back up to the top and start over. On Jimmy's fourth or fifth turn, he crawled inside the laundry basket and sat Indian-style with his head tucked between his knees, covered by his arms. Theresa crouched behind him and pushed him to the edge, then shoved him down the stairs. The basket thudded against the wall, and Jimmy realized mildly that a chunk of it fell into his lap, leaving a black gash in the wall. She bounded down the stairs after him, set him up against, then shoved him down the second flight, both of them red-faced with tears squirting out of their eyes from laughter. The basket then hit against something else, although he knew he was nearly a foot away from the front door. He lifted his head and found himself staring up at the shocked, horrified face of his mother, eyes wide and mouth agape. He stopped laughing immediately; Theresa had gone completely silent behind him.*

After that they were both grounded for two weeks, and were never allowed to stay home without a babysitter again. When they fussed and questioned why their mother wouldn't trust them, she looked at them with dismay. "When you show me you're both responsible enough to be by yourself, then we'll see."

"Jimmy, are you all right?" His mother's voice pulled him back from his thoughts. She gently touched his cheek, her eyes deep with concern. "Maybe you should go up and lie down for a while. You've been driving such a long time, I bet you're exhausted."

He had been driving a long time, but the truth was he didn't feel the least bit tired. He had reached the point of sleep deprivation when you try to close your eyes only to find them wide open a moment later. He gave her a reassuring smile and patted her hand away gently. "I'm fine, mom."

She looked uncertain but didn't argue; instead she took his bags and started upstairs. Family portraits lined the wall; the first of him at four with his left front tooth missing and his sister in pigtails, the one slightly above it with him in braces at twelve... Each one marked the changes of their family, but one thing remained constant; it was always just the three of them.

The upstairs guest bedroom had a yellow-musty scent and the air felt thick and un-breathed in the last ten years, but it was bright and homely with its butter cream walls, white down comforter on the bed, and antique lamps on the nightstand. She took the bags from him and set them on his bed.

"I know what you're thinking," she said with a light laugh. "My tastes are old-fashioned at best, but it should do for now, and you have your own bathroom this way."

"Does he know I'm coming?" Jimmy asked, still standing in the doorway.

He saw his mother's shoulders stiffen for a moment, then she continued to take his things out one-by-one, fold them, and set them in the drawers neatly. "I talked to Stacie today. Frank has to work and Abigail has come down with a touch of the flu, but she said she'd be here either today or Saturday."

"Mom," he said, now walking over to stand next to her. "Does he know?"

She sighed, finally giving in, and looked up at him. She suddenly looked very small, and very afraid. "Yes," she told him reluctantly. "He knows. I called him yesterday to tell him you'd be here. Jimmy, are you *sure* you want to do this?"

No, he wasn't sure he *wanted* to, but they knew he had come based on a *need to*. When his mother had called him the previous week to tell him his father's lung cancer had returned and they weren't sure how much longer he had, there was no question in Jimmy's mind that he *had* to see his father. There were things he needed to know, questions that had gone unanswered for too long.

He didn't answer now, but he didn't need to. She dropped her eyes again, folded and tucked away his last shirt, then straightened up. "Dinner will be ready soon," she said before she started to leave. "Get some rest."

"I thought I would go for a walk before dinner," he told her. "I've been sitting in that car for two days; I need some fresh air."

He saw her eyes clouded over with that worried fright, but she nodded and went downstairs without a word.

It was raining more heavily now, the drops collecting in small pools on the street, but he left without a jacket anyway. The rain felt cool and refreshing on his skin, he allowed the frigid air to fill his lungs, glad to be out of the thick, still atmosphere inside the house. He walked to the end of the street and turned left, heading down towards Tallulah Street.

A few years ago this was known as The Poor Side, and from the looks of it, it still was; townhouses and run-down apartment buildings that had been all but forgotten by the city and shunned by The Up-Towners. People who lived in these neighborhoods were mostly ones with low-paying jobs like janitors or waitresses or plumbers, or businessmen who never fully recovered from the crash of the economy. The kids from these parts were usually the ones most likely picked on at school. During the last few years Jimmy lived here, as bigger supermarkets started buying out the smaller business in town, the Olson's store began to suffer. Soon Mr. and Mrs. Olson had to sell the house they had lived in for the past fifty-some years and move to The Poor Side. It broke Mr. Olson's heart, but he was a stubborn man with a great deal of pride, and refused to ask for handouts.

Jimmy found himself standing in front of the dilapidated townhouse where the Olson's resided when he left home. The royal blue paint was chipped, in a few spots there were large, angry splotches of rotted wood siding. The gate squeaked loudly as he pushed it open and walked up to the front door. He knocked three times and stood with hands stuffed in his pockets. *What am I doing here? Of course they don't still live here. I'll just turn around and go back home...I'm leaving right now.* But instead, when there was no response the first time, he knocked again four times. Finally he heard footsteps drawing closer and the lock click open. A pretty, tall redheaded girl with blue-gray eyes appeared in front of him. She eyed him suspiciously, keeping the door halfway closed.

"Yes?" She asked, her eyes apprehensive and, he thought, slightly afraid.

"Oh, I'm sorry," he said dumbly, shifting back and forth uncomfortably on his feet. "I was – Well, I was looking for someone I used to know. A couple – Mr. and Mrs. Olson?"

"They're my mom and dad. Why are you looking for them?" She frowned thoughtfully, studying his face, then suddenly her eyes brightened. "*Jimmy? Jimmy Oversteen?*"

"Hi, Sarah," he said, smiling. *My, if you would have told me ten years ago that the freckle-faced, gangly little girl that used to chase me around the playground would turn out to be such a beautiful woman...* "Did your parents move? Where are they living now?"

She looked at him apologetically. "Jimmy... I hate to have to tell you like this, but mom and dad have been gone this past five years. Mom had cancer and we lost Dad to a heart attack six months later."

Despite how close he had been with them, he was surprised to find a lump growing in his throat as she said this. His stomach tightened into knots. He swallowed thickly and finally managed a barely audible, "Oh… I'm sorry…."

Several agonizing moments of silence passed before them before she spoke again. It couldn't have been more than ten seconds, but to Jimmy it felt like a millennium. She glanced at his wet clothes and dripping hair. "Would you like to come in? You can warm up, you're *soaked*."

He smiled at her again. "Like mother, like daughter."

She pursed her lips in a tight smirk. "I'll take that as a compliment, now come in before you catch pneumonia."

He laughed as she unlatched the screen door and let him inside. There was a dank, swampy smell laced with the scent of tobacco. In the days before people became aware of second-hand smoke it was normal for people to smoke inside, and it wasn't uncommon to see Mr. Olson in his beat up armchair, puffing on a cigar or his pipe. His chair was still there, along with the light yellow couch Mrs. Olson bought in Italy on their honeymoon, a little coffee table and armoire with a small TV. A stack of envelopes sat on the table, and as they passed to the kitchen, he saw the red OVERDUE stamped letters across each one, which explained why she was so wary of him when he first came to the door.

The kitchen was brightly lit, done all in light blues. She waved him over to the kitchen table, then grabbed the teapot and started to boil the water. He watched her out of the corner of his eye. She really *had* changed; her light blue jeans hugged the soft, womanly of her hips snuggly, the blouse she was wearing showing off a classy amount of cleavage, a sapphire cross necklace dangling above her breasts. She made small-talk for a while – he told her about being an architect and living in California – until she brought the tea over and set a cup in front of him. He thanked her and took a sip, the tea was overly sweet and burned his throat a bit, but it warmed him up immediately.

"After Dad had to stop working he and Mom lost everything. They did their best, but it was hard for them, then Mom got sick. Dad tried to take care of her, but it was too much for him and he had to put her in a nursing home. Without a pension and no income, he couldn't afford to get by let alone pay for all of her medical needs. My husband and I offered to help, but you know how stubborn he was."

"You're married?" He asked, cocking an eyebrow at her. There was no ring on her finger.

She smiled bitterly. "Divorced. Anyway, after Mom died I eventually convinced him to come and stay with my husband and I, but he was never the same. He just had no will to keep going, you know? Six months later he had the heart attack. I've always thought maybe that wasn't what really killed him; it was a *broken* heart." She blinked and seemed to remember she was talking to him, and laughed softly. "Sounds silly, I guess."

"No," he said. That excruciating silence fell between them again. He sat forward, putting his chin on his hands and narrowing his eyes at her thoughtfully. "So, divorced, huh? You got kids?"

"A little boy, Trevor, he'll be eleven in March," she said, picking absentmindedly at the tablecloth. "He lives with his Dad during the school-year, and then he stays with me during the summer. I think it's easier this way, while I stay here and try to sort out all of Mom and Dad's debt."

He nodded understandingly, "makes sense."

"So, what about you, Mr. Hot-Shot? Did you ever get married? Have kids?"

He stared down into his mug, fiddling with the handle. The topic of relationships always made him uncomfortable for reasons even unbeknownst to him. "No. I was seeing someone a while ago, but with work and everything..." He trailed off, unsure of how to finish.

He thought she would make a joke, but she didn't. Just looked at him sympathetically and nodded. "I know what you mean. Mom and Dad always made it look so *easy*. Fifty-three years and even near the end they still acted like they were on their honeymoon. They were so lucky to find what they had with each other." She paused to take a sip of her tea and brush a piece of her hair behind her ear. "They really loved you, you know. My dad thought of you like a son. They kept every Christmas card you sent. Mom even bought all those architectural magazines you were in when your career started to take off. How's your mom doing?"

"She's doing pretty well, I think. Tired, but she's all right."

"Are you just passing through?"

"I came to see my dad. He's dying."

She sat forward, resting her chin on her hands, listening intently.

"He has cancer and the doctors say it's spread too far for them to do anything about it. They really don't know how long he has. And it's…" He sighed and brought his hands down hard on the table, causing the tea to slosh around in his mug. "I'm almost thirty and I've never even talked to the man. I know my mom doesn't think it's right but it's something I feel I have to do."

She sat back smoothed out the rumples in the tablecloth. "I think it's a good idea."

"You do?"

"Sure. You know, I don't know how I would have gotten through these past years without mom and dad if I didn't have my memories of them. Everyone deserves closure, and if you feel like this is the way for you to get it, then you're doing the right thing. He *is* your father."

It suddenly dawned on him that being here with her was the first time he'd smiled since he got the phone call from his mom that his father was dying. "I've really missed you, Sarah."

"Well, maybe you oughta come around a little more often then," she said amiably, then laughed that sweet, throaty giggle.

"I should," he agreed. He glanced at his watch. "I should probably head back, Mom is probably wondering where I am." He got up and began to pick up the dishes.

She waved him away. "No, no. Don't worry about this; I'll take care of it." She followed him to the door. She leaned languidly against the doorframe. "It's good to see you again, Jimmy. Take care of yourself."

He lightly pecked her cheek. "Thanks for the tea, and the talk."

"Anytime," she told him, her cheeks slightly flushed.

He stuffed his hands in his pockets and walked down the steps to the walkway and headed toward the road. Before he reached the gate she spoke again.

"Jimmy?"

He turned toward her.

"I hope you get what you're looking for when you talk to your dad."

"Thanks," he said quietly, then stepped onto the sidewalk.

That night he lay in bed, his eyes aching to close but unable to sleep. Golden streaks of sunlight began to poke through the curtains just as he managed to drift off into a restless, troubled sleep. An hour later, he was awake again.

The next morning his mother was still asleep when he quietly treaded downstairs and left the house. It was another gray morning with sheets of dark clouds blanketing the sky. The houses in the neighborhood stood dark and quiet, the thick curtains and blinds shutting out the early morning light. As he drove by he noticed Sarah's car was gone. He remembered she said she was a waitress, and most mornings she had to get up with the sun to open. Just beyond her house the road curved right and he followed it.

Driving through the street he had lived on until he was nine felt like sinking into the ocean; the memories swam frantically through his mind, filling up his lungs until it was almost impossible to draw in breath. It was only until after he passed and began down Main Street again that he realized his knuckles were white from clutching the steering wheel. The house stood silent, shadowed by the increasing pink light of sunrise. A pink and white playhouse stood in the front yard next to a double swing-set, an abandoned tricycle was tipped over by the garage. Inside he imagined the people living there; a blissfully married husband and wife lying tangled up in each other's arms and white sheets, while a little girl and boy slept in the adjoining rooms, cozy and sleeping in pleasant dreams.

His eyes remained glued on the house as it passed until he had to crane his neck to see it. Lost in thought, he almost didn't see the little boy that flew in front of his car on a bicycle, just missing it by a few inches. He swerved quickly to the left and stopped at the corner. In the rear-view-mirror the boy's mother was hugging her son fiercely. She shouted something angry at Jimmy before dragging the boy back across the street, although he didn't hear exactly what she said. Jimmy folded his arms and leaned his head against the steering wheel as he tried to slow his racing heart. Suddenly his stomach felt as if he had just ridden a Tilt-A-Whirl at an amusement park about seventeen times, and for a moment he was sure he was going to be sick. Finally, slowly, he raised his head and released the parking break, pulled back onto the road and continued on.

The tall, sprawling building with its endless banks of windows was the only place in town that was not associated with any recollections for Jimmy. It conjured up no images of the past or brought any old feelings bubbling up to the surface – probably because this was the one place he had never been. After parking by the entrance he walked into the large, open lobby. He passed by the information desk; he knew where he was going.

As with driving here, instinct was leading him. He found the bank of elevators and took them up to the second floor. All was quiet except for the quiet shuffle and hushed murmurs of nurses on their morning shifts. Florescent panels of light washed over his face, casting him in ghastly, exhausted shadows. Out of the corner of his eye he saw the nurses whisper something in each other's ear as they watched him cautiously, but none of them came over. Jimmy walked through the door at the end of the long hallway and paused before pushing the door open without knocking.

The hospital room was small, with a flowered border along the dusty pink walls. A blue rocking chair sat by the window. A silhouette outlined by the light turned the chair slowly toward the door, and he found himself face-to-face with his father. For a minute Jimmy stood frozen, dumbfounded and unsure of what to do next. In his mind he expected to see a cardboard cut-out of that old, grainy photograph he'd stolen from the chest in the attic, but what he found was a full flesh and blood man with gray, thinning hair and skin like the hide of a leather wallet. A century seemed to pass between them, both of them unmoving and unvoiced. At last, the man slowly got to his feet with the aid of a dark wooden cane with a handle molded to his hand. Jimmy realized how small and frail he was, and for a moment he was sure his legs would give out underneath him and he would have to dart forward to catch him. He made it over, however, and stood in front of Jimmy, studying his face closely.

"Hi, Jim," his father spoke first, his voice a gravelly, feeble croak.

"Hi, dad," he answered, the words came out in a cracked, hoarse whisper. He cleared his throat against the back of his hand.

His father motioned for him to sit down, then hobbled back to his rocking chair. Jimmy sat across from him and once again they stared at each other in silence. Before this trip Jimmy never realized how much he hated silence.

"Your mother said you were coming."

"I wanted to see you."

He drew in a deep breath and spoke: "Why?"

His father set the pitcher down slowly and looked at him, his eyes uncomprehending. "'*Why?*'" He repeated the question, puzzled.

"Why did you leave?" He clarified, not taking his eyes away from his father's eyes. He hadn't intended to blurt the question out this way, but it tumbled out of his mouth before he had a chance to stop it.

His father took his time sipping his water, then set the glass beside him and looked back at Jimmy with his hands folded. "You look good, Jimmy. Your mother tells me you've made quite a name for yourself as a… uh, architect, is it? You've done real well."

Jimmy narrowed his eyes. "Why did you leave us, dad?"

"Jim…" His father sighed. He always hated that nickname. "There are just some things you don't understand, all right? Sometimes a man does what he has to do."

"No matter who gets hurt in the process?" Jimmy snapped bitterly. "I'm a grown man, dad, so don't treat me like some naïve little boy. I asked you a question, and I want an answer; I think I *deserve* one, don't you? Now, tell me. If I don't understand, then please, enlighten me."

He saw something in his father's eyes then that he wasn't anticipating; complete astonishment. Jimmy realized he had caught his father totally off-guard. But, what was he expecting? Did he sincerely expect Jimmy not to ask?

"Things were different when your mother and I got married, Jim…"

"Stop calling me that," he interrupted sharply.

There was that look, the one of a man who has been suddenly ambushed by a tribe of cannibals in the middle of the jungle. He continued slowly, the ice in his glass clanking as he shook them around. "We were just out of high school, and I wasn't planning on having a wife and family at 19 – neither of us were, to be fair. The town was going through hard times, money was tight –"

"So, you took the easy way out and ran away," Jimmy finished darkly.

"As I said; I did what I had to do," he replied defensively, then sat back and gazed out the window passively. "That's no way for kids to grow up."

"And growing up without a father is?" He countered vehemently, his arms crossed over his chest. He knew he was acting petty, but he didn't care – He came all this way for answers, and he was going to get them one way or another.

"You have a point," his father admitted. Jimmy thought for a moment he would continue, but he just sat there, twiddling his thumbs idly.

"If you don't want to answer that, then I have another..." He said, trying to sound more diplomatic. "Why didn't you ever come and try to see Theresa and me? Even if you and Mom split up, we were your children and we didn't do anything wrong, so there was no reason for you not to want to be a part of *our* lives."

"Your mother wouldn't allow it," he replied simply, as if Jimmy should have known all along.

"That's a cop-out and you know it. She may have kept you from seeing us, but you never even *tried*."

For the first time since they began talking, his father smiled; it was a small, crooked smirk that Jimmy didn't like. "There's a lot that your mother hasn't told you."

"Then why don't *you* tell me?"

"Jim –"

"I told you not to call me that."

"Jimmy," he corrected himself, then waited for Jimmy to nod his approval before he continued. "A year after your mother and I finalized our divorce, when you were five, I filed for custody of both you and your sister, but she refused and forced me into a settlement outside of court, along with an order that I never try to contact either of you ever again."

He didn't believe him. It was absurd; why would his mother try to keep his father from seeing him? To protect him maybe, but she had to have known that for a boy, growing up without his father could only hurt him in the long-run. He remained quiet this time.

"When you were thirteen I tried again, even came back here so I could see you. But again, your mother refused to even let me speak to you over the phone. Because of our agreement, her lawyers told me that if I tried to contact you, I would have to give up my parental rights to you completely. After I left, I tried to send you letters, but your mother must have destroyed them, and I lost track of you completely when you moved."

Jimmy stared at his father, stunned and speechless. Someone had just taken a hammer to everything he ever believed, and he found himself frantically trying to discern the pieces and put them all back together again. When he was a child, he discovered if he was having a particularly terrible nightmare, all he had to do was shut his eyes tightly and count to ten. A moment later he would find himself floating back to consciousness, discovering he was in his bed, and the horror of his dream was safely locked back into his subconscious mind; he was back in a world where everything made sense. He wished he could do that now; he wished to close his eyes and find himself back in his apartment in Los Angeles, the images that haunted his dreams far away on the shores of imagination. He realized he actually had closed his eyes when the hospital room and his father's face swam back into focus.

"I know you don't believe me," his father said, for the first time actually sounding apologetic. "You have no reason to. There's no excuse or reason I can give that would be good enough, and there aren't enough ways to tell you I'm sorry. But, whether you choose to believe it or not, I did try and I wanted what was best for you and your sister. I know it's too late now, but you need to know that."

Neither of them spoke for a long time after that. Throughout the rest of the morning they rode on top of the peeks of conversation before dropping off into even longer valleys of nothing. Eventually he glanced up at the clock: 12:45.

"I should go," he said quietly, beginning to stand up.

"Before you leave, I have something for you." His father stood and walked to the small set of drawers next to the bed, fumbled around until he found what he was looking for, then shuffled over to where Jimmy stood by the door. The old man flattened his sons hand, then laid a pocket-watch; the case was gold with small engraved designs around the edges. On the back were his father's initials: T.J.O.

"I know I should have been there, so this is for you, so you'll remember where you need to be before it's too late."

"Thanks, dad," he said. He put his hand out and his father shook it firmly before Jimmy left.

With the two suitcases he brought in the trunk and his father's watch in the pocket of his jeans, jangling against his side as he walked, he walked back through the hospital and out into the brisk air afternoon breeze. Tall trees swayed and danced in the sunlight, and everything suddenly seemed brighter. He left the window down as he drove through town, taking everything in one last time as the cool air flowed around his face. As he past beyond the town limits he glanced in the mirror, watching as his childhood home receded farther and farther away.

An hour later he was back on the freeway, heading toward California. The pocket-watch dangled from the rear-view-mirror, glinting and winking in the sunlight. As he drove away he turned up the radio and began to sing along.

Radiance

Through all the pain
An endless rain,
More losses than gains.
Her light inside
Will always shine.

Her radiance

After tattered dreams and broken lies
Nothing but the darkness to hear her cries.
Her inner strength will never die.

Her radiance

With beauty, dignity, and grace
The rainbow she continues to chase.
A heart of gold and fingers of lace.

Her radiance

After the struggle, after the fight
Her fire will still be burning bright.
She'll always have her inner light.

Her radiance

Introduction – The Summer Series

The First of Autumn and *Coffee Shop Barista* are a part of a series about a young girl named Summer whose life is changed when a young man unexpectedly enters her world. The parts were written independent of each other, however they are all part of a longer story that is still in the works.

The First of Autumn

Summer trudged down the flight of stairs leading to her apartment and began her twenty-minute trek to the community college. The dry, fallen autumn leaves crunched beneath her feet as she walked. The heels of her boots clicked rhythmically in time with her steps. It was a clear September day; the bright sun warming her back and casting long shadows on the pavement, gray and muted in contrast to the deep cranberry and rich golden shades of Fall. Despite the warmth of the sun, a sharp chill in the breeze stung her cheeks and nipped harshly at her nose. She shivered as she pulled her pumpkin colored scarf over the lower part of her face and wrapped her arms tightly around herself. Adjusting her bag across her shoulder, she continued walking. Her messy blonde curls were bouncing underneath the hand-knitted wool cap that she tugged down snuggly over her ears.. Everything seemed in motion; changing, turning, shifting with the season. Even the birds chirping in the trees above were in transition, preparing to migrate to warmer climates before the deadly frost of winter.

As she rounded the corner at the end of her street, a sudden gust of wind shook the branches of the large maple tree that stood in front of her. The leaves trembled as a single one broke loose and floated down where it stuck to the top of her hat. Reaching up and feeling around, she plucked it off, twirling it between her fingers as she inspected it closely. The sharp edges were just beginning to turn a deep raspberry shade, although in the center it still held on to its natural emerald green.

Lifting the flap of her bag, she carefully tucked the leaf inside her worn, flimsy leather journal. She wasn't sure what use it would be to her, but she was sure she could find some purpose for it in her art class later that afternoon.

Before walking the three remaining blocks to the school, Summer turned a second left toward the sorority house where her best friend, Kelli, had taken up residence last semester. As she ventured down Cinder Street, she could almost feel the palpable shift in atmosphere, and in her mood. What had possessed Kelli to make the move to this notoriously dangerous and unsanitary side of town in favor of a sorority where the sisters were better known for their drunken-fueled parties than for their academic achievements, Summer still couldn't figure out.

The Kappa Beta Zappa house stood at the center of the block. The run-down, brick building looked awkward in the middle of prominent Victorian homes with their quaint wrap-around porches and intimidating cylinder pillars standing in the entryways.

Sloppy, indecipherable spray-painted letters covered the entire left side, no doubt the artistic expression of the aforementioned fraternity brothers at one of the weekend 'get togethers'. Ebony shutters framed each of the windows which didn't seem to match the number of floors, some of them chipped and warped from harsh winters and blatant neglect. A few of the windows had no panes at all, while others had been shattered by baseballs thrown by the children in the next door apartments. The sisters had fixed the problem by carelessly tacking a random, scrap piece of plywood across the gaping holes.

Garbage littered the steps leading up to the large, heavy royal blue doors, both of which had no locks and the left one could not be opened from the outside. A curious red stain marked the rug just inside the door, and Summer shuddered as she considered the possibilities of its origin.

Standing in the foyer, it was hard to believe that human beings actually inhabited lived there. Beer bottles and Bud Light cans, dirty dishes, empty, greasy pizza boxes, randomly discarded articles of clothing. Carefully stepping around the disgusting mess she made her way quietly through the war zone that was the living room. She ascended the carpeted stairway that creaked and groaned under her feet, threatening to give way.

One of Kelli's sisters lay sprawled out in the middle of the hallway, her messy black hair splayed out around her face, lips slightly parted as she snored, allowing a single trickle of saliva to cascade down her chin. She came to the third door with the names of the girls who slept there across the door on glittery pieces of construction paper.

Finally, she knocked on the door.

Coffee Shop Barista

Summer sat in her usual spot in the back room of the coffee shop, idly twirling a strand of her long, blonde unruly mop of untamable curls. In her frenzied rush earlier that morning, she had quickly thrown it into a messy bun, not bothering to brush it or detangle it. The early autumn drizzle caused the mess to frizz making it sticking out every which way around her face. She sighed and pushed it out of her eyes. Her legs swung back and forth as she sat perched on the tall stool in the corner. A light blue pillow padded the hard, cold metal seat that wobbled unsteadily as she rocked; each stool leg was taped carelessly by a thin strip of duct tape, barely hanging on by the screws. She looked out the window, broken by a baseball bat that had smashed through the glass and bounced all the way out to the counter in the front of the shop. Streams of sunlight shone through the spaces between the boards that had been sloppily slapped over the hole, providing just enough room to navigate the otherwise completely dark room. On the shelves large jumbo-sized cans of espresso and coffee beans stood next to containers of small cups of cream, extra filters for the machines and bags of sugar.

The Butterfly Paperweight

"Those snobby three-piece suit businessmen just have to have sugar in their coffee," she muttered bitterly.

Though not much to look at, this room was the only quiet place in the entire shop where she could escape. And escape she needed from the demanding costumers and Tara, the black-haired, bubble gum popping, telephone talking cosmetology student. Besides the patrons, Tara was Summer's only companion on Sundays; everyone else had conveniently scheduled social lives, leaving her to single-handedly run the shop and refrain herself from throwing sharp objects at Tara.

Her thoughts were interrupted by the sound of the bells on the door chiming melodically, signaling someone's arrival. Reluctantly, she pushed herself off the stool and walked out from the darkness of her room to the brightly-lit coffee shop. Then, she saw him.

He had been coming into the coffee shop where Summer worked for the past two weeks. Every day at precisely 1:30PM he came strolling in wearing a graphic t-shirt with a band, or a witty phrase on the front and faded light blue jeans. A baseball cap always pulled down over his dark eyes, his dark blonde, slightly shaggy hair spilling into his face. Summer hurried out to the counter before any of her co-workers could get there first. She had been waiting for him, although she'd never admit to it if someone asked her. She immediately began mixing his Grande Spiced Pumpkin Latte. It was what he always ordered, so by now she didn't need to ask.

As she poured the milk into the mixer she discreetly turned the napkin holder or the silver sugar containers lightly to the left so she could watch him without blatantly staring. The lower part of his face was softly rounded, his features delicate with a subtle cleft chin, plump, full lips and wide, slightly up-turned nose. He stood patiently as he waited, his hands stuffed into the pockets of his jeans, one knee slightly bent as he rocked back and forth on his feet, glancing around at the artwork.

Summer realized that while she was staring, she had totally lost focus of the task at hand and had almost overflowed the Styrofoam cup with milk. Quickly she pulled the jug up and twisted the cap back on, trying to maintain a look of casualness as she finished the coffee off with a dollop of whip cream and a sprinkle of cinnamon. She tried to steady her suddenly shaky hands, attempting to hide the deep blush that had begun to creep up her neck, heading for her cheeks.

Thank goodness it had been a particularly hot summer. She had taken full advantage of the heat, laying out in the sun for several hours and taking extra long runs in the morning, providing her with a perfect cocoa tan and a great cover-up.

"Here you go," she said quietly, smiling shyly at him. For once, she was glad she couldn't see his eyes. That would only make it worse.

Her words seemed to snap him out of his thoughts as he studied a knock-off of Van Gough's 'Starry Night' that hung on the farthest wall near the restrooms. His head snapped to attention and he flinched slightly. "Oh, thanks," he said smoothly, his lips stretching into a wide smile, revealing a set of perfect pearly whites. Summer felt her heart do a sudden, quick flip-flop that made her a little dizzy.

He reached into his back pocket and pulled out his beat-up leather wallet, taking out $4.50 and handing it to her, reaching out for the cup. As he grasped the cup Summer marveled momentarily at how his large hands dwarfed hers. They were warm as they lightly brushed her palm, causing a shiver to go up her spine. He took his coffee and retreated to the last table near the window, as he walked Summer took notice of the lazy, comfortable swagger in his steps. He slid into one of the chairs and sat his coffee before him, pulling out a small notepad and pencil from his pocket, he flipped to the first empty space and began to write. Every now and then he would pause to take a sip from his cup or to run the end of his pencil across his full lower lip thoughtfully as he stared out into the parking lot.

Summer deposited the money into the cash register, noting that he had once again slipped her an extra $5.00. She found herself making every excuse to stay out in front while he was there; the filter in the brewer needed to be changed, the sugar needed to be refilled, the small plastic cups of cream needed to be restocked. All the while she would continue to briefly glance over, holding her gaze just long enough to watch him as he sat hunched over the table, his elbows resting at the edge, his chin resting on his knuckles. His arms were toned, although not overly muscular like most of the meat-head jocks at the college. Once his coffee ran out, he pushed his chair back and stood up slowly, pulling at the back of his shirt that had ridden up as he sat. He strutted over to the trash can nearest the counter and tossed away his cup. He bunched the napkin up into a tight ball in his hands and tossed it into the trashcan near the door, pushing the door open as the bells on the handle chimed. Before leaving he turned his face back toward Summer, offering another bright smile and a short wave of his hand, then turned and stepped out into the bright, crisp afternoon.

As she watched the sunlight wash over his back, his arms swinging languidly at his side, something inside tugged at her heart, churning and wrenching her stomach.

She shook her head as she turned toward the back room.

*You **really** need to get out more, Summer,* she thought to herself.

Should We Be
By: Joshua Rheaume and Kayla Meyers

It's the season of love and everywhere I see
Hearts falling down, shattered fantasies
The sky grows dark as romance gets colder
Broken lovers cry out, "is the dream over?"

Are we fools or just too clever, to end up like them
Are we better off saying we're just friends
It doesn't mean that we don't feel, we just know better

Should we follow the example of others
Forsaking honesty for what they believe
Should we be lovers?
Should we be lovers?

This is an unfinished song written by Joshua Rheaume and myself. Once it is completed we hope to record it as a duet and put it up on his website along with Before You.

Phantasmal Beauty

"Yes, mom, I promise I'll call as soon as we land," Destiny said, wrinkling her forehead as she strained to hear what her mother was saying over the dodgy reception of her cell phone. She struggled to get her shoes off and put them on the conveyer belt along with her jewelry and carry-on bag, careful not to bump into anyone else in line going through security at the Chicago International Airport.

Behind her a bald, grouchy-looking man in an expensive suit cleared his throat loudly as he gave her a dirty look.

She gave him a quick apologetic smile and put the phone back to her ear. "Okay, mom, I have to go now. No, it'll be okay, just trust me. I'll talk to you soon, okay? Love you, bye," she hung up and stepped through the metal detector.

After getting through security, Destiny threw her bag over her shoulder and made her way down to gate A112 where she would board the flight that would take her to New York and then on to France. On the way she stopped at the Starbucks to get a white chocolate mocha and a bagel. At the terminal she found a seat facing the window and sat down to watch as the maintenance crew did a last minute inspection of the plane before the checked baggage was loaded. Nibbling on her bagel, she took out a book her mother had given her on the history of Paris and began to read.

The airport was exponentially filling up with people as the morning wore on and the lazy sun poked its head above the horizon, throwing marmalade streaks across the hazy violet sky. Destiny randomly glanced up from her book to people-watch and cogitate on her fellow passenger's stories; young newlyweds about to venture off to some tropical destination for a leisurely honeymoon, and the elderly couple on their way to Reno where they would proceed to gamble away their retirement. A businessman rushed by hurriedly, nearly tripping over her things as he talked using his blue-tooth earpiece. With a grunt of frustration he kicked her bag out of the way and kept going, promising the person on the line that he *would* be home for his son's fifth birthday no matter what it took. And there she was, eighteen-year-old high-school senior Destiny Faith Landers, who should have been home filling out cap and gown orders and sending graduation invitations was instead moving halfway around the world to a country because someone had promised to fulfill a childhood dream.

It happened a month ago on an unexceptional Saturday during a typical shopping trip to the mall, not exactly the place or time you expect an once-in-a-lifetime opportunity to present itself. She was standing in the Teen Clothing section of Macy's when an inconspicuous man in casual, slightly rumpled garb sidled up beside her.

"Excuse me, young miss," he said in a thick French accent. "May I have a moment of your time?"

"Huh?" She grunted as she looked up in surprise. "*Me?*"

"Yes," he replied in a low voice, coming a little closer.

In school the first thing you're taught is to never talk to strangers, and this guy definitely looked like a long-time card-holding member of the Creepy Old Men club. Natural instinct told her to scream and run as quickly as she could. However, her mother *was* standing nearby looking at some lipstick by the make-up counter, so if he tried anything she could easily call for help. Slowly, she turned around to face him.

"Um…what?" She asked while taking one step away from him hoping the message was clear.

He nodded deferentially and kept his distance. "My name is Gianni Tupello," he introduced himself cordially, reaching into his gray jacket and producing a business card.

Destiny hesitated, and then slowly accepted it. She read the black, bold letters in bewilderment:

Bellissimo Bellas International Model Agency
Gianni Tupello – Agent

Before she could ask questions, he continued. "You see, I am here because we are in desperate need of fresh, young faces to represent our agency in the fashion industry. My associates have entrusted me with the laborious task of coming to America in search of undiscovered talent and bringing the most promising girls I find back to Paris with me."

The Butterfly Paperweight

"Oh, well, I'm sorry to burst your bubble, but you've got the wrong person. I've never modeled before, unless you count strutting up and down the hallway in my winter formal dress in front of my mother and sisters..." She paused, her eyes widening. "Wait, did you say *Paris*, as in, *France?*"

He laughed heartily, his thin face stretching into a wide grin. "I certainly did, mademoiselle," he confirmed. "And despite your inexperience, you are by far the most stunning young lady I've happened across during my time here. With a little grooming and the right people to guide you, all of which you will be provided should you choose to accept this offer. I think you have an enormous amount of potential."

"Des, honey, who are you talking to?" Her mother came over, stepping beside Destiny like a mother lioness protecting her cub from a predator. "May I help you, *sir?*" She asked coldly.

"Beg your pardon, Madame," He tipped his fedora and bowed. "I was just discussing a career opportunity with your daughter. As I was saying--"

Without letting him finish Destiny's mother began pulling her away. "She's not interested, I'm sorry. Goodbye, mister."

Destiny tried to wriggle from her mother's tight grasp. She twisted around and watched his slight form being swallowed in the crowd of people.

"Good day, then, mademoiselle," he called after her before she lost sight of him completely.

"Honestly, Desi, you really need to be more careful about who you speak to. You don't *know* that man, what if he tried something with you? *Please*, tell me you didn't give him any personal information."

"No, mom, don't worry. I didn't tell him anything. Sorry, you're right," she mumbled, following her mother outside to the parking lot.

Suddenly, she remembered the card he'd given her. She was still holding it. Keeping it out of her mother's sight, she turned it over in her hand and inspected the back. Printed in scrawling handwriting was an address, date and time. The card instructed that she be at 87260 E Adams St. at 2:30 PM on Wednesday, May 26th.

Persuading her best friend Laura to skip her Honors Human Psychology class during the last week of school to give her a ride wasn't easy. She reminded her about the vow Laura made to repay Destiny for the night she rescued her from a party where she'd gotten deliriously drunk. She then covered for Laura the next morning when she awoke with a hang-over. Laura caved pretty quickly. They snuck out during study hall and headed for Chicago.

"Remind me again why I'm driving you to this random place in the middle of downtown Chicago when I should be in class finishing up my final project?" Laura asked as they drove along toward the city.

"Last week I met a man at the mall," she explained a little sheepishly. Despite telling herself that she had to follow her gut-instinct that it was for real, there was still enough room in her mind for doubt. "He's a scout for a modeling agency in Paris, and he's in the States looking for new talent."

"Wait a minute, back up," Laura interrupted as they halted at the stop sign before heading south on the highway. "This dude is from *Paris* and he came to Chicago, Illinois looking for models?"

"Why not?" Destiny asked.

"No offense, Tiny, but we don't exactly have a ton of Giselle Bundchens walking around Chicago Place Mall," Laura pointed out. "I mean, if he wanted to find gorgeous women, there are eight hundred million different places I can think of, like California or New York."

"Gee, thanks a lot," Destiny grumbled, staring out the window as they maneuvered through downtown, passing by Millennium Park and the Art Institute of Chicago.

"You know I didn't mean it like that. If I didn't believe you I wouldn't even be doing this." Laura asked, glancing sideways at her friend.

"No, I guess you wouldn't. I do really appreciate this, you know."

"I know you do," Laura said, then grinned impishly. "And you're going to show me how much you appreciate it when you go as Ben's date for the prom along with Caleb and me."

"Say *what?*" She turned around to face Laura, horrified. Ben was Laura's boyfriend's younger brother, a sophomore in high school. "Oh, no, I will do *no* such thing. You couldn't bribe me to go with him if you offered me a million dollars."

"Well, if you've changed your mind…" Laura shrugged, pretending to turn the car around.

"Stop it, Laura!" Destiny yelled, grabbing onto the wheel and holding it steady. "Don't even think about it. Fine, I'll go with Ben, just don't expect me to hang around with him at the dance all night. Andy is having an after party and everyone is going, I refuse to be the only girl to miss it because my date got sick after his idiotic friends dared him to drink all the punch."

"How generous of you," Laura said, then sat back with a contented smirk.

The rest of the drive was silent. This part of town was mostly abandoned factories and long-since-closed-down paper mills, rapidly decaying neglected buildings and dirty streets. Chicago's homeless wandered the streets, seeking somewhere to sleep. Besides the wanders and pigeons, there wasn't a living soul. It seemed unfeasible that just a few blocks away the city's elite were seeing plays and symphonies for $80 a pop at Civic Opera House.

"Gosh, this looks like a fabulous neighborhood, Tiny," Laura remarked sarcastically. "While I would love to stick around for tea, I forgot my pepper spray and I don't think I like the idea of dying before I'm voted prom queen,"

"Knock it off," Destiny told her, watching the addresses on each building. "Here it is on the left."

Laura turned the car off. She stared at the gray, three-storey building. "Are you sure *this* is the right place? It doesn't look like anyone's been here since the Eisenhower administration was in office."

"It's the right place," Destiny confirmed as she unbuckled her seatbelt and got out.

"You're just going to go traipsing around in there all by yourself? What if this guy is some kind of ex-con serial killer who's just escaped from the mental institution and is out for young female blood?"

"You really need to lay off the Stephen King novels, Laura, they're starting to destroy the last brain cells you have left," Destiny said. "I'm just going inside to look. If

I don't see anyone I'll come right back." She dug in her purse and produced a rubber fish on a keychain, a gift from her little sister. There was a small light inside the fish's mouth that illuminated when you pushed its sides. "Look, if I run into trouble I'll shine this out the window to signal for help."

"You got it, Batman," Laura agreed, sitting back.

"I'll be right back," Destiny promised as she turned and started to walk away.

"Beware of ghosts...and cockroaches!" Laura called after her.

Destiny shot her laughing friend a disgruntled glare before stepping over the threshold and inside. The overly-spacious room, which Destiny assumed had once served as a waiting area, was completely empty save for a couple pieces of furniture in the corner that were so age-worn and mottled that it was hard to distinguish their original color. A desk sat collecting dust against the far wall, a broken service bell and disconnected telephone on top. Clumps of dirt littered the hardwood floor. It smelled dank and stale. Cool air flushed through an open vent in the ceiling, making a quiet hissing noise. There was no one.

She sighed deeply in disappointment, throwing away the card in a waste basket by the door. All the way here she had told herself she wouldn't be upset if this happened. Yet now she was on the brink of tears. Her mother's voice echoed in her ears, *I told you to listen to me, Desi....* She paused suddenly and cocked her ear toward the stairwell going up to the second floor. Footsteps clicked across the ceiling above her followed by voices. *Beware of ghosts!* Laura reminded her. Turning back, she walked across the room and began up the stairs. At the top, a set of heavy doors stood closed bearing a sign that read: *QUIET PLEASE*. Destiny hesitated for a moment, and then went inside.

The doors opened to another large room, with mirrored walls and ballet bars. On one side photography equipment was set up. Just behind the cameras, three people sat quietly deliberating and conferring with the photographer.

The man she met in the mall the week before was busy talking. Twelve girls formed a line on the other end of the room, waiting for their turn with the photographer and interview with the judges. All of them were all tall and thin (some downright skeletal), and each was beautiful in a different way. Some had thick portfolios with headshots and professional pictures. Others looked as if they, like Destiny, had no idea what they had gotten themselves into. The girl that was presently talking with Mr. Tupello and his two companions had long raven locks, almond-shaped cobalt eyes and legs up to her waist. The girl Destiny had nearly run over when she walked in had spiky red hair and heavy, dark makeup.

Mr. Tupello looked over as the door lock closed down with a hollow click. He smiled broadly and waved 'hello' at Destiny. She smiled back at him in embarrassment and then sheepishly waved back at Mr. Tupello. Moments later he approached her.

"I'm so glad you could make it, Ms…" he trailed off, raising his thick eyebrows inquisitively.

"Destiny Landers," she said with a smile.

"Ms. Landry, I'm very pleased to see you. Is your mother with you?" He asked, glancing over her shoulder.

"Um, no, I got a ride from someone…"

"Ah, I see, very good. Well, good luck," he said, then went back and took his place behind the cameraman, leaning over to whisper something to his comrade while another girl posed in front of the white backdrop.

Destiny was the last girl to go up. She walked in front of the backdrop and stood there, slightly awkwardly, in front of the bright lights and cameras.

"What's your name?" The woman scout asked slightly rudely.

"She is Ms. Destiny Landers," Mr. Tupello interjected before she could answer.

The photographer set everything up while Mr. Tupello gave Destiny instructions – look to your left, put your right hand on your hip, cock your leg to the side, don't smile, now smile. She did as she was told, ignoring the sharp pain in her eyes from the blaring lights. Once they had all the information they needed Mr. Tupello stood up and shook her hand. It seemed like an eternity before the shooting was over. She answered a few basic questions and it was over.

"Thank you for coming. We'll be in touch," Mr. Tupello told her.

The woman, named Judith Walter, gave her a look that said she wasn't impressed by her act.

Destiny took her time leaving, trying to inconspicuously eaves-drop on their whispered conversation.

"Too awkward in front of a camera," Mr. Centrilli, the third person of the trio, said in dismay as he marked something of on his rap-sheet. "She's not even close to being ready, and we don't have six months to start training her."

"And she may be tall, but she's not small-boned, either," Judith added, shaking her head. "If she's even going to consider going into high fashion she'd need to lose at least ten pounds to start."

"But, something about her is extraordinary, don't you think? We've been across this country. I have yet to see the spark in any girl's eye that I find in her. She's going to be something very special, and we're going to deeply regret it if we're not the ones who discovered her."

Destiny grinned to herself, closing the door she made her way downstairs. Laura had probably already called the police to say her best friend had been eaten by the undead ghouls haunting E. Adams St. She was halfway outside when she heard Mr. Tupello calling after her. As she turned she saw him come huffing and puffing down the stairs.

"Ms. Landry... I just wanted to..." he let out a long, heavy breath and swallowed thickly. "To welcome you to Paris."

"Oh my god, are you serious?!" She shrieked excitedly, her eyes widening in surprise.

"If your mother agrees by the end of next week you'll be flying first class on your way to fame and fortune."

She covered her mouth and screamed then flung her arms around Mr. Tupello's thin frame. "Thank you so much, Mr. Tupello! And don't worry, I'll work it out with my mom, I promise. Thank you!"

The Butterfly Paperweight

After much conversation and many disscusions and reassuring from Mr. Tupeello, Destiny's mother relented. On May 31st 2008, Destiny packed all her things into two small bags, said goodbye to her tearful mother and younger sisters.

Her mother called at least five times on the way to the airport. Destiny had done everything she could to reassure her that everything would be fine. But, inside she was all butterflies. She had no idea what to expect living in Paris. Were the people there going to be warm and receptive, or would she be perceived as just another American looking to soak up the glamour of being internationally famous? Could she even *handle* the demands of the fashion industry, especially as someone fresh out of high school?

She glanced up at the clock – another thirty-eight minutes before her flight boarded. Dog-earing the page she was reading she got up and wandered over to the little gift-shop. After plucking up an issue of *Vogue* and *Cosmo*, she went over to a vending machine and debated the all-important decision; Doritos or Pringles. She stood there for a long time with one hand on her hip, the other tapping her chin thoughtfully. Finally she settled on Salsa Verde Doritos and headed back.

When she got to her spot she found someone in her chair, hunched over her book and rummaging through her carry-on bag. Running over and snatching her things from the young man's hands, she glared angrily at him. "Excuse me, what in the hell do you think you're doing?"

"Oh, I'm sorry," he said in an Italian accent. Wisps of his dark hair fell into his chocolate brown eyes as he stood. "I saw your things and I –"

"Took it as an open invitation to go through my bag," she interrupted with a contemptuous scoff, moving her stuff one seat over and plopping down with her back to him.

He scooted over to her and looked over her shoulder. "I'm very sorry, miss. My name is Jacques Catonelle." He surveyed the magazines in her lap. "You like beauty," he commented. "Are you a model?"

"What's it to you?" She snapped, whipping her head around to look at him.

"I was just going to say that I can see why," he said quietly after the silence. "Being a beautiful woman yourself, it makes sense that you admire pretty things."

Despite being irritated by him, she couldn't stop the blush that crept into her cheeks. "Thanks," she replied. She twisted around in her chair and extended her hand to Jacques. "I'm …"

"Destiny Faith Landry," he finished, accepting her gesture with a gentle handshake.

"You found my ID?!" she gaped at him in horror.

"Your bag was lying there, I thought it was misplaced so I was going to find who it belonged to so I could take it over there," he nodded to the main desk.

Destiny slanted her eyes at him in suspicion.

"Honest!" He promised, making a cross on his chest.

"So, what else did you find out about me?"

"You wear Maybelline Pink Diamonds lip-gloss, MAC eye shadow and Heavenly Victoria's Secret hand lotion," he recited with a slight air of self-satisfaction.

She frowned a little. "I didn't bring any hand lotion with me, with the new airline regulations you're not allowed to bring any liquids onboard the plane."

"I know," he said, grinning at her with a twinkle in his dark eyes. "You are wearing it. My mother wears it also – you smell like her."

Destiny's mouth fell open in astonishment, hot blood rushing to her face. "*What?* You – Why, you insufferable, unbelievable –"

Just then a female voice came faintly over the intercom: "Flight 801 will now board first class passengers only."

She jumped to her feet and grabbed her things as quickly as she could. In her rush she dropped her book.

Jacques leaned down and picked it up, holding it out to her. "Maybe we will meet again, Destiny Landers.

"*Ugh!*" She groaned in disgust as she grabbed it and stormed off.

In line with the other first class passengers Destiny stood there and chewed her nails as she always did when she was anxious or upset. She was still fuming.

"Are you okay?" An elderly man standing behind her asked kindly.

She jumped a little, startled by the sudden intrusion into her thoughts. "Oh, yes," she replied. "Yes, I'm fine. I just haven't flown since I was young, and I guess I'm a little nervous."

"Flying can be a little scary if you're not used to it – *Anything* that's new to you is daunting," he agreed, nodding understandingly. "When I was your age I was terrified of planes, my family never traveled because we didn't have the money, but then after high school I decided to go to school in Phoenix, Arizona. Of course, to get there from Augusta in South Carolina I had to fly. At first I almost backed out and went to a school near my hometown, but then I started thinking about what a great education I'd be missing out on plus the experience of being on my own. That doesn't mean I wasn't still afraid, but I wanted to go so badly that I decided to face my fear. You see, you have to teach yourself to focus on the destination and not how you're getting there. I'm sure there's something great waiting for you wherever you're headed."

"Yes, there is," Destiny said with a smile. "Thank you."

He smiled and patted her arm. The line moved and she handed the lady her ticket, then boarded the plane.

Unspoken

Staring after you as you leave again,
I bid the words to come but I never speak.
I call after you, scream inside my head
Broken promises that will never be said-
Like I want you, I need you.

Tie a noose of silence around my neck.
Momentary release from the pain
Of all the lies I've told myself,
To make it through the grayness of the night
'Cause you're the colors of my world
All that brings my soul to life-
And I won't lie.

So close to you in these million yards of space.
I reach out to you, but you're so far away.
Phantom fears surround my heart, choking off my breath
So I can't even say
I covet you, I desire you.

Why can't you talk to me?
Don't you think I know, I'd understand.
Imperfections are what is beautiful.
No pretty words, not a fantasy,
All I want is what's real.
And while I know this, I will never say
That I dream of you, I love you.

Saving You

Oh, I can't stand it anymore
All these walls around you.
Can't break them down, can't get through,
These bricks and jagged stones
Crush my heart and break my soul.
And I don't know how you can't see
Your walls are killing you, destroying me.

Last night I dreamed of saving you-
Saving you, saving you from yourself.
Pushing back the blackened waves that lick your face
Oh, sometimes I dream of saving you, saving you
But I can't get through to you.

Treading water and I fall so deep
Into the abyss of your heart.
I gain some ground before it gets too steep.
We go 'round and 'round, still we never go that far.
And still I dream.

At night I dream of saving you-
Saving you, saving you from yourself.
Breaking the waves that crash around your face-
Oh, just wish I was saving you.
Saving you from yourself.

And I'm sorry, I'm sorry.
It has to be this way, I don't know why.
But I can't live this way hanging in the void
Of your indecision.

So for now I'll just dream of saving you.
Oh, in my dreams I'll be saving you, saving you.
And maybe by saving you
I'll save myself, too.

Cycle

He loves me, he loves me not.
I'm waiting here love, though you seem to have forgot.
Plucking the supple petals from a daisy
So delicate, see how they buckle and give so easily.

Where are you love? I seem to have forgot.
The wilted roses strewn about our path,
See how they fall and die so fast.
It's the season of love, the foliage has changed.

The trees have grown, love has been forgot.
In the dead mulch and tangled weeds I have gotten lost.
During the season of love, the world begins to turn
And the forest yearns and it burns.

In the wreckage love is forgot.
So for restoration and rebirth
I'll plant the seed and sew the earth.
And next season the rain will come,
And love will grow and spread around.

Acknowledgments and Thank Yous

My mom and dad - I don't know what I would do without you. If it wasn't for your unconditional love and support I would have never gotten this far. You are the greatest mom and dad anyone could ask for. I love you more than anything.

My brother, Jason – You have been the biggest male role model in my life for as long as I can remember. You are the perfect example of integrity, strength and dedication in every aspect. I'll never be able to tell you how much I admire and look up to you. I am so proud of you for all you've accomplished. I love you.

My twin brother, Spencer – Without a doubt, you are the most important person to me. You are the center of my world and without you there is no way I could find the strength to go on. We've been through so much together and with every year that passes I find myself relying more and more on you for support. No matter what happens, remember that you will always come first to me. I am so proud to call myself your twin sister. I love you so much.

Grandma – No words could ever say just how much you mean to me. You have been so special to me from the time I was a little girl, you've taught me so much and made me who I am today. Despite how difficult things can get in my life I know I can always lean on you for the comfort and love that I need. I would be lost if you weren't in my life. I love you with all my heart.

Uncle Tim and auntie Alyson – I cannot find the right words to thank you enough for everything you've done for my family and I all our lives. Throughout some of the hardest times you have been there for me to help in any way you could and lend all your love and support. You both mean the absolute world to me. I love you!

My extended family – Your continuous love means so much to me. Thank you for all you've done, I love you.

My friends, local and around the world – Thank you so much for being there for me through everything these past few years, I couldn't have made it this far if it weren't for you all. I love you guys so much!

Joshua Rheaume – You are one of the best friends and writing partners that I could ever ask for. Out of everyone you were the first person to take a serious interest in my writing and offered me such great encouragement and support in my journey to get published. I love everything we have created together, and I can't wait to see what else our friendship will produce in the future. Thank you for believing in me and giving me the faith that anything is possible.

Lindsay Preston and WritingRoom.com – No matter how many times I say "thank you", it still doesn't seem to be an adequate way for me to express my deepest gratitude for what you've done for me. I could have never found a better company to work on my first book with, and I feel so privileged to be the first of many writers to publish a book with PublishingRoom. Lindsay, you are so wonderful and it has been a total honor to work along side you. Thank you so much for believing in me! I am the luckiest girl in the world.

Printed in the United States
128489LV00001B/12/P